The Junior Novelization

Library of Congress Control Number: 2008922360
ISBN: 978-0-7364-2496-7
www.randomhouse.com/kids/disney
Printed in the United States of America
10 9 8 7 6 5   First Edition

The Junior Novelization

Adapted by Irene Trimble

Random House New York

One morning, the lights of a pet shop flickered to life, followed by the sound of keys unlocking the front door. Soon voices filled the air, awakening a litter of puppies. The pups raised their heads and blinked their tiny eyes open. Tails wagged and wet noses pressed against the glass as the day's first customers wandered in.

But one puppy paid no attention. This little white ball of fluff had his eyes fixed on a smiling carrot chew toy in the corner of his pen. The fur on the puppy's back rose as he slowly sized up the carrot. He growled, crouched down, and in one fierce jump attacked the plush vegetable.

With the carrot locked between his tiny teeth, the puppy rolled onto his back and shook his head from side to side. Then he noticed a red-haired girl smiling at him. The puppy stood and stared back. He dropped the carrot and out of the corner of his eye saw something wagging behind him.

He spun around and barked, leaping to catch his own tail. The girl giggled and turned to the shopkeeper.

"That one!" she said, laying her hand on the glass. The puppy waddled over and pressed his paw to her hand. There was no doubt about it: They both knew they were a perfect match.

The shopkeeper took the fluffy white puppy from the pen and placed him in the red-haired girl's arms. "You're heavy!" she said, giggling as the puppy licked her face. "And slobbery!"

The little girl fastened a brand-new collar with a shiny tag around the puppy's neck. She kissed the top of his furry head.

"You're my good boy," she said, nuzzling her new best friend.

Five years later, the little girl, Penny, answered her cell phone. The puppy, whom she had named Bolt, was standing loyally right next to her, now fully grown. Bolt's white fur sported a distinctive black lightning bolt mark on his left side.

"Penny," a man gasped on the other end of the line. "I don't have much time."

"Daddy?" she asked. "Are you okay?"

"Something's come up at work, honey," he answered quickly as dark shadows slowly stalked him in the alley where he was hiding. "Daddy is not gonna be home for a while. You can't go back to the house, Penny. I don't want you to go home."

"What's happening?" she cried. Bolt's ears perked up in alarm.

Penny's father hastily hung up the phone. As the shadowy figures overtook him, he recalled the night he had genetically altered Bolt, giving the faithful dog amazing powers. Bolt would be able to defend Penny, even against their most powerful enemies.

"It's okay," he had told Penny. "You won't be alone. You have Bolt. He can protect you now."

Atop the roof of a downtown building, Penny stared through a pair of high-powered binoculars. She was determined to find her father and rescue him. Bolt was next to her, focusing his keen canine senses in the same direction. Penny was searching the building across the street, listening to conversations with the binoculars' high-tech hearing device as she scanned the offices.

Through one window she finally spied the back of a bald man's tattooed head. He was talking to a menacing figure projected on a large floating screen. The man on the screen had one green eye, and a cat perched on his shoulder. Penny recognized the man on the screen immediately. It was the evil Dr. Calico—the man who wanted to steal her father's valuable scientific formulas for his own sinister purposes.

"There he is," Penny said to Bolt. She lowered the binoculars so Bolt could take a look. Bolt growled. Penny understood—the dog hated the bad guys who threatened to do harm to good people.

"Any luck getting our guest to spill his guts?" she heard Calico's henchman ask.

"Oh, his guts will spill," Calico sneered. "One way or another."

"Never!" Penny recognized her father's voice. "I'll never talk!"

Penny zoomed in with the binoculars to see her father on-screen behind Calico. He was bound to a chair. A cat was curled at his feet, hissing.

"Daddy!" Penny whispered. Bolt's ears stood up.

"You are beginning to irk me, Professor," Dr. Calico replied. "I am irked, and that will not do." Calico looked enormous on the screen as he turned to face his henchman, who was watching and listening in his office. "Has the package arrived? I think it might make our dear friend a bit more . . . communicative."

The henchman turned to another small figure in the office and nodded. "I'm sending an asset to pick it up."

"Gorgeous," Dr. Calico replied. "Have him bring it to me on the first flight."

The floating screen disappeared, and one of the henchman's thugs exited through the area made vacant by its departure.

Penny and Bolt were already on their way to finding Dr. Calico—and saving her father.

Penny and Bolt waited on a street corner for Dr. Calico's henchman to make his next move. Penny peeked over the magazine she was pretending to read. She saw a man emerge from the building and coolly walk down the street. Penny gave Bolt a nudge. "Let's go," she whispered.

The two raced down the alley, but there was no one there. They were staring at a dead end. Suddenly, cage doors slammed down behind them. They were trapped!

Two headlights flashed on. A black sedan at the end of the alley revved its engine. Penny and Bolt heard the sickening sound of tires squealing as the car roared toward them, but there was no place to go, with the steel bars of the cage blocking them on one side and a solid brick wall behind them!

Inside the dark sedan, one of Calico's thugs looked at his boss's cruel face on a screen in the dashboard.

"We only need the girl," Calico said calmly. The driver grinned and slammed down on the accelerator, causing the car to race forward, heading directly toward Penny! The girl ducked low, hoping to protect herself.

Bolt immediately stepped out in front of Penny. Fearless, he lowered his head level with the oncoming chrome bumper. Then, like a tightly coiled spring, he shot forward at terrific speed and head-butted the sedan off the ground.

Twisting in the air, the dark sedan landed on its roof, trapping the driver. Seeing the driver wiggling to get free, Penny walked over to the steaming wreck and politely tapped on the window.

"What!" the driver growled, lowering his window.

"Where's Calico?" Penny demanded

The driver turned his head. "I'm not talking to you," he replied, refusing to give away Calico's location.

Bolt and Penny exchanged a look. They had their way of dealing with these kinds of situations.

Moments later, Bolt had them out of the alley and was dangling the sedan over the edge of a bridge. The car's chrome bumper was locked firmly between his incredibly strong jaws.

"Bolivia!" the driver screamed. "Bolivia! Calico is in Bolivia! Near Lake Rogaguado!"

"Lake Rogaguado," Penny said, shaking her head. "I should have known."

Out on the bay, attack choppers appeared on the

horizon. They were moving in fast. Penny nodded to Bolt, who set the sedan back up on the bridge. She pulled a compact object out of her backpack and swiftly began unfolding various different parts. It was a scooter! Putting on her helmet, Penny stepped onto the set of wheels and started moving.

"Let's go," she said coolly as the attack choppers cut through the sky.

Penny and Bolt raced over the bridge as the evil Calico's helicopters swooped down and began chasing them.

Penny flipped on her helmet's digital viewfinder. "Bolivia," she said, scanning the screen's data. "There's a flight leaving in ten minutes!"

One of the choppers zoomed down, dropping a team of motorcyclists armed with gloves that emitted electric jolts. These were Calico's shock troopers.

Penny gunned the scooter, but the shock troopers were too fast.

"Bolt!" she shouted, calling for help. "Zoom!"

Bolt got the message. Penny pushed a button on her handlebars and a rope burst from a secret compartment. Bolt grabbed the rope in his mouth. His paws dug into the asphalt as he launched forward. In a blur of motion, he and Penny rocketed away.

Darting through traffic and under trucks, Bolt pulled Penny along at lightning speed. Penny looked over her shoulder. The shock troopers had picked up their trail again.

The little girl and her dog made a sharp left turn, speeding into an old warehouse. The motorcyclists roared right behind them.

Penny and Bolt were headed for a dead end—a wall was directly in their path. Bolt didn't slow down for a second. Ahead of Penny's scooter, he lowered his head and—*CRASH!*—smashed through the building, bringing Penny safely along behind him.

Penny heard the sound of motorcycles behind them crashing into the wreckage Bolt had left in his wake. She looked over her shoulder and laughed. She knew that these were bad men who would hurt not only her but also her father.

Bolt and Penny raced from the warehouse onto the freeway. Penny checked her watch. If they hurried, they could still make the next flight to Bolivia.

Penny looked at a tanker truck in front of her. Its shiny metal reflected the shock troopers still behind her. One of Dr. Calico's motorcyclists was weaving in and out of traffic, getting closer and closer. Penny heard the roar of his powerful black bike as he pulled up alongside her. She saw the trooper toss a bomb onto a gasoline truck on a highway below them.

"Bolt!" Penny called out, pointing to the bomb on the truck. "Fetch!"

Bolt swiftly peeled away from Penny, leaping from

the overpass to the highway below, just as a school bus pulled up next to the truck. Bolt ran right up to the truck. The kids on the bus waved and shouted, "Puppy!"

Bolt knew he had to get that bomb!

The kids watched Bolt leap onto the gasoline truck. He grabbed the bomb in his teeth. Now he needed to get rid of it, and that required a plan. In a flash, Bolt was running beside the guardrail, easily passing the bus and all the cars. He spotted a crane with a wrecking ball next to the freeway. A speeding train moved in the opposite direction—toward Penny.

Bolt formulated his plan. Jumping from an overpass, he landed on the wrecking ball and swung down onto the train. He would take care of two things fast—safely getting rid of the ticking bomb in his mouth, and rescuing Penny, who was being chased by more shock troopers.

Suddenly, Bolt skidded to a stop on top of the train—one of Calico's helicopters was chasing him. Bracing his legs, he stared hard at the chopper. Red-hot lasers flashed from Bolt's eyes, burning through the chopper. Just before its smoking engines failed and it tumbled out of sight, the chopper dropped a motorcycle atop the speeding train.

Ready for attack, the motorcycle's rider fired a couple of tracking missiles. Bolt leaped off the train, the missiles following him no matter which way he turned.

Bolt looked back toward the freeway for Penny, the bomb still ticking in his mouth. He spotted her struggling to escape the powerful electric jolts from a shock trooper's gloves. Bolt looked at the huge chasm that separated them—just as another helicopter rose from its depths, ready to fire.

Bolt hurdled over the helicopter, dodging its spinning, chopping blades. The tracking missiles followed Bolt and hit the chopper instead of the dog! Bolt's timing was perfect. As the chopper exploded, Bolt landed on the other side of the huge chasm and jumped onto the motorcyclist who was chasing Penny. With one swift move, Bolt placed the ticking bomb on the trooper's head.

In a panic, the shock trooper grabbed the bomb and tossed it skyward, hitting the other attack chopper. As the exploding chopper filled the sky with flames, the trooper smacked his head in disbelief—*ZAP!*— knocking himself out with his own electrified glove!

With Bolt back by her side, Penny revved her scooter and spotted a sign.

"Airport!" Penny said excitedly, reading the sign to Bolt. They were almost there! But an army of Calico's vehicles and helicopters blocked their path.

"Uh-oh," Penny muttered, knowing they only had minutes to make that flight to Bolivia and find her father. It was time to unleash Bolt's super bark. She screeched to a halt and shouted to Bolt, "Speak!"

Bolt moved into the special stance that was required to bring the greatest power to his super bark. He focused on the massive amounts of machinery in front of him and thought about one thing: protecting the little girl behind him. He let out a bark of such force that it blew the vehicles off the ground and ripped the pavement with the might of a hurricane. They landed in a twisted, fiery heap. The way to the airport was now clear.

Penny let out a big sigh and took off her helmet. She reached into her backpack and pulled out an instant camera. She knelt down beside Bolt, held the camera up, and took their picture. Bolt licked her face. "Okay, okay. Good job, buddy!" Penny said.

Bolt beamed at his smiling owner. Penny held the picture in her hand, proclaiming, "That's a keeper!" She lifted Bolt into her arms and gave him a quick snuggle.

Penny seemed relaxed, but Bolt was still on the alert. He needed to keep Penny safe!

Bolt could speak to, and understand, other animals. But he did not understand human language beyond basic commands. So he did not know what Penny knew—that all this time, they were being filmed for an episode of a TV show! Even now, everyone on the set would not move until Bolt was safely inside his trailer with Penny.

Then and only then would the crew members emerge from their hiding places. The actors would relax, and the motorcyclist stuntpeople would stand up and dust themselves off. They were all working on a sound-stage in Hollywood, California—a make-believe set created just to shoot the TV show. All the people were actors—the bad guys, Penny, her father . . . even Bolt!

Penny carried Bolt across the wreckage. Bolt looked around at the destruction, still worried about Penny's welfare.

"It's all right, tough guy," she said, trying to calm him down. "You got 'em all!"

Bolt wagged his tail and barked as Penny climbed a set of stairs that led into a trailer with his name on it. The stage bell rang, and the director called, "Cut!" That meant that Bolt was out of hearing distance. The crew of the hit TV series *Bolt* got to work.

"All right," the stage manager shouted. "Let's clean this mess up."

Inside a control booth, the director and his crew stared at the day's filming. They watched Penny and Bolt zip through their action sequences—motorcyclists flying, helicopters exploding nicely. Then, as the camera zoomed in on Bolt's big bark scene, the whole crew slumped in frustration. They could all see the piece of sound equipment above Bolt's head, and they knew the shot was ruined.

The boom-mike guy cowered in the back of the

control booth as the director shouted, "That's sloppy! The dog could have seen that. He could have *seen* that!"

A slight woman stepped forward. "Um . . . who cares if the dog sees a boom mike?" she asked.

"Forgive me for answering a question with a question," the director said flatly, "but—who are you?"

"Mindy. From the network," the woman answered.

The director nodded and rolled his eyes. He pointed to the monitor. "Of course," he said quietly to himself, fuming. "Let me ask you, Mindy-from-the-network: What do you see here?"

"Uh . . . the dog," Mindy replied flatly.

"'The dog,' she says," the director sighed. "Oh, Mindy. Poor, poor Mindy."

"Am I missing something?" Mindy asked impatiently.

"YOU'RE MISSING EVERYTHING, MINDY!" the director shouted, out of control. "You see a dog. I see an animal who believes with every fiber of his being— EVERY FIBER—that the girl he loves is in mortal danger. I see a depth of emotion on the face of that canine the likes of which has never been captured on-screen before. NEVER, Mindy-from-the-network!"

Mindy was getting a little annoyed with the lecture. But the director's passion escalated as he continued explaining his way of working: "We jump through hoops to make sure that Bolt believes everything is real. It's why we don't miss marks. It's why we most certainly don't let the dog see boom mikes! Because, Mindy-from-the-network, if the dog believes it, the audience believes it."

There was a long pause as the director stared hard at Mindy. And she stared right back.

"Wow. Okay. Well, you want reality? Here you go, chief." Mindy-from-the-network suddenly seemed to find her voice. A very loud voice. "The show's too predictable. The girl's in danger. The dog saves her from the creepy English guy. WE GET IT! THERE'S ALWAYS A HAPPY ENDING!" she barked. "Our focus group tells us eighteen-to-thirty-five-year-olds are not happy. So maybe you should spend a little less time worrying about the dog's acting and more time figuring out how to stop twenty-year-olds in Topeka from changing the channel—because if you lose so much as half a rating point," Mindy threatened as the crew stared slack-jawed, "I will fire everyone in this room." She pointed at the director. "Starting with you! How's that for real?" she said, turning curtly on her heel and slamming the door behind her.

Inside Bolt's trailer, Penny was busy pinning up the photo she'd taken earlier. The trailer wall was covered with photos from past episodes of their show. There was no sign of cameras or microphones or stuntpeople in any of the photos. Bolt saw them all as real. His and Penny's life on the show was always real for him, and he was always on the alert, ready to protect Penny from the green-eyed man and his cats.

"There," Penny said cheerfully. "You saved me again, Bolt."

Bolt didn't look. He was still vigilant, guarding the door.

Penny scratched his head. "You got 'em, Bolt. No one's gonna hurt me." But Bolt wouldn't move from his protective mode. "Bolt, look at me. I'm fine, see?"

Penny frowned and took out one of Bolt's doggie toys. "Come here, buddy. Come here."

Bolt wouldn't budge. Penny tried tossing a ball, but he just ignored it. "Yeah, that one's no fun, either," Penny said, adding the ball to a pile of dog toys in the corner. Then she noticed the old smiling carrot from his puppy days. She grabbed it and waved it around. "What do we have here?" she said, giving the toy a squeak. "Your old buddy Mr. Carrot, see?"

That seemed to catch Bolt's attention—but just for a moment. His eyes darted toward the carrot toy, but he still stood fast.

Penny's cell phone suddenly buzzed her a new text. She read the message, got up, and walked toward the door.

Bolt stepped in front of her and began to whine. Penny looked into his big brown eyes. "Bolt, you know I have to go." She kissed him on the top of the head just as she had done when he was a puppy. "You're my good boy," she said, sadly closing the door behind her.

Outside Bolt's trailer, Penny saw her agent and her mom waiting.

"There's the little superstar!" a blond man in a sleek suit said, walking toward Penny. It was Penny's agent, hurrying her along to a photo shoot.

Instead, Penny rushed up to her mother. "Mom, I want to take Bolt home this weekend."

Penny's mother seemed hesitant. "Well, I, um, well, that would be—"

"Yeah, that would be nice," her agent interrupted. "That would be nice. That would. A little girl and her dog. Nothing better than that."

"So I can bring Bolt home?" Penny asked eagerly.

The agent knelt down and smiled at Penny. "As a friend, I say yes. But as your agent," he said, motioning to the soundstage, "I have to remind you this is Bolt's world. He has to stay here. Right here. Okay? Let's go."

Penny glared at him. "But he never gets to be a real dog! And it would only be for the weekend! And I—"

Before she could finish, her agent gave a fake smile and said, "You know what? It's a fair question. It is. And let's do this: Let's put a pin in it!"

Penny watched him pantomime sticking an invisible pin into the air. "Boop!" he said as if he'd performed an amazing magic trick. "Pin in! Now let it hang there a bit, and we'll readdress it when we've thought things through! Okay? Okay!"

Penny frowned. "I don't need to think it through! I want to take Bolt home!"

With a wave of his hand, her agent signaled to the hair and makeup team standing near Bolt's trailer.

"Look at this face," he said, still smiling at Penny. "I have a little girl at home, the love of my life. I would do anything for her," he continued as he addressed Penny. "And I'd trade her for you in a heartbeat. True story. Now, that reminds me, we should get to wardrobe."

Penny was heartbroken. "But I . . . I just—"

Her agent was determined not to allow her to take Bolt home. Penny turned to face her entourage, which included a makeup artist, a hairstylist, and a photographer. She looked from one face to another as the group whisked her away from the set and Bolt's trailer.

Two cats from the day's shoot immediately slinked back onto the empty set. Their eyes glowed in the darkness as they anxiously approached Bolt's trailer. The chubby beige cat was a newcomer to the show. He had lots of questions for the black cat, who had worked on the show almost as long as Bolt.

"So the dog thinks this is all real?" the new cat asked.

The black cat nodded toward the trailer and laughed. "This guy never leaves the set. It's unbelievable. Whenever I get the chance, I find this is the perfect way to unwind. C'mon. Follow my lead."

The two climbed the side of Bolt's trailer and peeked through the open skylight. "I like to start with an evil laugh," the veteran cat actor said, letting out a maniacal howl.

Bolt bared his teeth. "Hello, hairballs," he said, boldly facing his enemies. To Bolt, all cats were Dr. Calico's evil minions, out to hurt Penny.

"You may have won today, Bolt," the cat replied in a deep, threatening voice, toying with the dog. "But in the end, we will get your little Penny."

"Not likely, cat, for you have chosen to follow the path of evil," Bolt said firmly. "Ultimately, it will destroy you, along with your evil puppet master!"

The two cats shared a delighted look. "Wow," the new cat whispered.

Laughing, the black cat lowered his voice again and spoke to Bolt. "She's a goner, dog. The green-eyed man has a plan, and soon he will execute it!"

"And then he will execute her," the new cat chimed in, starting to enjoy antagonizing the dog.

Bolt looked up at the skylight. "I've got a little message for you to take back to your green-eyed man. You tell him his old friend Bolt says—"

The black cat interrupted Bolt. "Is it long?"

"Is what long?" Bolt asked.

"The message. Is it a long message? Because I have a horrible memory."

The new cat muffled a laugh.

"I'll make it brief," Bolt said. "You tell him—"

But after a bit, the black cat held up a paw. "Whoa! Way too many words! I was like, 'What?' And then I was like, 'Huh?' And then," he said, turning to his buddy, "I got bored. Something about 'clutches'?"

The black cat turned to leave, saying simply, "I'll do my best."

But the newcomer cat lingered, telling Bolt how much he admired the dog. "Big fan. Love your work. Love you!"

"Come back here," Bolt demanded, "you, you sick, fuzzy, box-littering little—"

The two cats trotted back to their carriers and stepped inside. "Dogs," the black cat said, chuckling.

"Cats," Bolt grumbled, settling back into his watchdog position in front of the trailer door.

Filming began bright and early in the morning. Bolt and Penny were racing through the Bolivian jungle. Or at least, Bolt thought so.

The crew members were carefully camouflaged to blend in with the jungle set so Bolt would not see them. The director and the entire crew were making sure that Bolt had no idea that the jungle, the actors—the drama of his whole life—were fake.

The camera followed Penny as she pointed to a truck with Dr. Calico's symbol on its side. She and Bolt crept under the truck and rode on its axles to infiltrate Dr. Calico's lair.

As soon as they were inside the high-tech compound, Bolt could hear the sounds of heavy boots approaching. Bolt and Penny made a run for it, dashing into Dr. Calico's secret lab. They carefully crept down a hallway, sticking to the shadows.

Sneaking through the ventilation shafts to avoid Dr. Calico's minions, the pair got a good view of the compound without being seen. Quietly, they moved through the air shafts, peeking down into different rooms, seeing various henchmen—and cats—at work for Calico. Bolt used his amazing strength to bend the metal bars that blocked their path. (He had no idea that the "metal" bars were really made of rubber.)

At last Penny spotted an enormous computer buzzing with electricity. She gasped. It was Dr. Calico's central computer. "If we can access it, we'll finally learn where they're keeping my father!"

Penny's eyes narrowed as she looked at three guards near the computer. Bolt could take care of them. From their hiding place, she flicked a penny (her signature coin) along the floor. It landed at the feet of one of the guards. The guard paused for a moment and then leaned down to pick it up. In a flash, Penny snapped her fingers and Bolt leaped out, ready for action. Within seconds, Bolt had knocked out two of the guards using his special karate chop.

Bolt didn't see them landing safely on cushions behind the scenes. The hidden crew was doing its job well.

Bolt and Penny crept up behind the final guard. This one would be hard to take on. He was armed with a rifle.

"Bolt, stare!" Penny shouted, knowing that Bolt understood that command all too well.

Bolt froze, his eyes fixed on the guard's rifle, thinking he was using his devastating heat vision to destroy the weapon.

"Now," the director whispered to the special-effects coordinator, who flipped a switch. The prop rifle exploded—or at least, it appeared to explode. Everyone but Bolt knew that it was just a special effect, and the fallen actor playing the guard was unhurt.

Penny let out a sigh of relief and jumped into a chair in front of the computer. Her fingers danced over the keyboard as she searched for clues to her father's whereabouts.

Then the lights in the compound blinked off. She and Bolt were suddenly in total darkness. Bolt's protective instincts kicked in. He could sense that they were not alone.

10

"**S**uch devotion," cackled a voice from a hole in the ceiling. "It brings me to tears."

Bolt immediately recognized the man behind the voice. It was Dr. Calico, no doubt surrounded by a swarm of evil cats.

"Your father's discoveries could be of great use to our organization," he hissed. "I'm sure he will be more accommodating now that I've got his lucky Penny."

Steel restraints on Penny's chair instantly clamped down on her arms and legs. She struggled to break free as a helicopter whirred overhead. It was shining a blue light down on Penny, now helpless in the chair.

A blue pod lowered from the helicopter, enclosing Penny. She screamed to Bolt from inside the pod, but it was no use. Bolt watched, barking with all his might, as his beloved Penny was lifted into the helicopter.

And then . . . she was gone.

The director turned triumphantly and gave Mindy-from-the-network a smug smile. They watched Bolt bark, frantic to get Penny back. "How did your focus group feel about cliffhangers?" the director said. "You want eighteen-to-thirty-five-year-olds? I'll give you eighteen-to-thirty-five-year-olds."

An animal trainer dressed in special protective gear grabbed Bolt from behind and placed him in a carrier. Bolt was frantic. He barked and barked, thinking that Penny was in trouble and he needed to rescue her!

Back on the soundstage, Penny could hear Bolt barking. He was calling for her. She tried to run over to him and show him she was safe. "It's okay, Bolt," she said, almost in tears. "I'm okay!"

But the director yelled, "Oh, whoa, whoa, whoa! Guards, stop her!"

Two stuntmen turned and grabbed Penny. "Hey, hey, hey! Hold on!" one stuntman said, holding her back.

"Listen to him," Penny pleaded, struggling to get away. "He needs to know I'm okay."

Penny's agent suddenly appeared on the set and took over. "No, you're not okay," he said firmly. "You've been kidnapped by the fiendish Dr. Calico. At least, that's what the dog needs to think." The agent smiled. "Just think how excited he'll be when he saves you tomorrow!"

Penny looked up at her agent. "But he's going to be freaking out all night. Please, just—"

"Wait a second. What's that behind your ear? Is that a . . . yes, it is! It's a pin!" the agent said to Penny. "Let's do this: Let's take the pin and put it in this conversation. Boop! And we will not take it down, no, ma'am, until this matter is resolved. You know what that reminds me of? The DVD release junket! Let's get going. It's a big push."

The agent ushered her along to a pack of anxious assistants and stylists who stood ready with their brushes and combs.

"I'll need at least ten minutes," the hairstylist said.

"Yeah, and I'm gonna need another twenty minutes in wardrobe," another said.

"Don't forget to mention the soundtrack," an assistant told Penny.

"All right," the agent said, pleased with himself. "Let's not crowd the talent. Step back. Step away."

But all Penny could hear was poor Bolt barking, wanting to rescue her from a make-believe villain.

Stan, the animal handler, struggled to get Bolt into his trailer. The dog was fighting fiercely, and Stan knew why. Bolt believed that it was his job to rescue Penny.

Watching Bolt through the trailer's skylight were the two cats from the set, ready as ever to tease Bolt into a frenzy. The cats had no idea what had just happened. They were preparing for another fun exchange with Bolt that would provide them with that evening's entertainment.

"I've been working on my evil laugh," the rookie beige cat said to the black cat. But the noise he made sounded awful. "It's not very good right now," he added.

Bolt heard them. He looked up. To Bolt, they were Dr. Calico's evil minions. He needed to get to them in order to find Penny. Desperate now, the dog scrambled right up Stan's body, climbing him like a ladder before he launched through the skylight.

"Aaaaah!" the cats screamed.

"Hey!" Stan shouted. He opened the trailer door and yelled to some of the other crew members, "I need help!" Then he called out, "Bolt! Come back!"

Bolt did not look back. He raced into the Bolivian jungle set, looking for Penny. He thought it seemed a little different. There was no one there. Dr. Calico must have left and taken Penny with him. But where?

"Hold on, Penny, hold on!" Bolt shouted. He retraced his steps to Dr. Calico's computer station, but it was dark and deserted.

"I'm too late!" Bolt said to himself, sniffing anxiously around the computer.

Bolt's ears suddenly perked up. Far in the distance, he could hear Penny's voice saying, "Bolt! Help!"

Following the sound of Penny's voice, Bolt scampered into an office corridor off the set. He skidded past an editing room, where a tired man was looking at a little screen. From the monitor came the words "Bolt! Help! Bolt! Help!"

Going too fast, Bolt raced past the editing room and finally slid to a halt just beyond the mailroom. He thought he had caught a glimpse of something. Sure enough, he backed up and looked through the mailroom and out the window. There it was—the pod that Dr. Calico had used to capture Penny! It was sitting atop a truck outside, well within Bolt's reach if he used his super strength and his super leaping abilities to burst through the window.

Bolt raced into the mailroom and jumped from one box to another to get to the window. Certain that Penny was trapped in the pod outside, he launched himself toward the window with all his might. But all his might was no match for a window made of real glass.

Bolt smacked his head into the thick glass and was knocked out cold. He fell into a box filled with hundreds of small pink packing peanuts. When the mailroom guy sauntered in moments later, he did not see Bolt passed out at the bottom of the box, hidden by the packing materials. The mailroom guy sealed the box and shipped it out.

Bolt's real adventures were about to begin.

The next morning, a shipment of boxes arrived at a large brick warehouse. A shipping clerk noticed one box out of the corner of his eye. It was shaking and rocking, about to tip over.

"Huh?" the clerk said, walking over to take a closer look.

He cut the box open and Bolt leaped out in a cloud of pink packing peanuts.

"Whoa! Hey!" the clerk called out, but Bolt jumped out an open window and was gone.

Bolt dove into a dirty alley and raced toward the street, searching for Penny. He screeched to a halt when he saw a man sitting on a bench reading a newspaper. The man was wearing a dark suit that seemed familiar. "The green-eyed man!" Bolt gasped excitedly.

There was a chain-link fence between Bolt and the nasty villain. But a chain-link fence was no match for Bolt! Or so he thought. He charged the fence. *BANG!* Bolt's head crashed into the metal mesh, leaving him stunned for a second. Recovering, Bolt quickly found a way around the fence and sneaked up behind the man on the bench. Swiftly, he lifted his paw to give the man one of his powerful karate chops. It didn't work. Bolt's paw almost slipped away from the man. The man turned, and Bolt looked into his face. The man had no green eye. In fact, he was not the green-eyed man at all!

Completely confused, Bolt took off down the crowded street, sending pedestrians scattering out of his way.

"Get outta here!" one yelled angrily.

Bolt was losing his patience. He scanned the crowd, shouting, "Penny? Penny!"

He had no idea that Penny was all the way across the country. Bolt had been shipped overnight from Hollywood to New York City!

Bolt ran until he came to a road construction site with barriers and signage to prevent people from entering the area. The pavement was broken and blocked with traffic cones. But Bolt didn't slow down. He knew he could easily jump the large chasm.

Confidently, he leaped into the air. But instead of sailing across the open space, he found himself tumbling into the hole. He climbed out awkwardly—with an orange cone stuck on his head.

Through the opening in the cone, Bolt spotted Dr. Calico's blue pod on the back of a flatbed truck.

"Penny!" Bolt shouted, shaking the orange cone off his head.

"Target acquired," he said to himself. He sprinted directly into the truck's path. "It ends here," Bolt said to the truck barreling toward him.

The driver hit the brakes, and the truck came to a stop inches from Bolt's head. Bolt saw the blue plastic chamber fall from the back of the truck.

"Penny!" Bolt raced toward the chamber as the door flipped open. But the only things inside it were a toilet and a roll of toilet paper.

Bolt stared into the empty toilet in the chamber and tilted his head. "Penny?" he asked, confused. Where was Penny? She had been sitting on a chair and enclosed in a blue pod just like this when Calico had taken her.

"They moved her!" he said. More determined than before, Bolt took off down the street. He had to find Penny.

Bolt ran, searching for Penny on every street corner and in every doorway. Finally, he spotted a group of dogs on a stroll with their walker.

Hoping for some information, he ran up to the pack and panted, "No time for formalities, brothers. My person is in danger, and—"

Bolt spun around to find a dachshund sniffing at his rear end. Bolt was shocked!

"What are you doing?" Bolt asked, horrified.

The dachshund backed away apologetically. "Oh, I'm sorry. Did you want to sniff mine first?"

Bolt felt something snap onto his collar. He turned to see that the dog walker had clipped him to a leash.

"Hey there!" she said. "Are you lost, sweetie?" All she heard was frantic barking from the poor pup.

Bolt broke away, sprinting off and dragging the leash behind him. "Hey! Wait!" the dog walker yelled as Bolt ran blindly, crashing into a pile of neatly stacked newspapers next to a magazine stand.

With a sheet of newspaper wrapped across his face, Bolt couldn't see a thing. He charged forward, running headlong into a wrought iron fence. The newspaper flew away from his face as Bolt was finally forced to stop, his head solidly wedged between the fence's bars. He tried to pull his head back, but it was no use. He looked up at New York's towering skyscrapers.

"Why can't I bend these stupid bars?" he asked himself as he pulled against the fence. He had bent plenty of metal bars before. Sure that it must be the work of some unknown evil force, he yanked his head back harder.

"Yo, buddy," said a pigeon standing on the ground. "You got your head stuck pretty good, huh, guy?" The pigeon, whose name was Vinnie, cocked his head, interested in the dog.

"Hey, guys! Come here!" Vinnie called out to a couple of pigeon buddies. "Check this out! He got his melon stuck!"

"Yup," another pigeon named Joey agreed. "That is one stuck melon."

Bolt shook his head, trying to bend the bars.

"Hey, hey, buddy, take it easy," Vinnie told him.

"I will not take it easy, pheasant," Bolt told the pigeon. "I'm missing my person!"

Vinnie shrugged.

"Hey, buddy, relax." The pigeon tilted his head to the side and pulled it back. "Like this," Vinnie said. "Turn and pull."

Vinnie quickly demonstrated again. "Turn and pull. Forget-about-it. You'll be out in no time."

Bolt followed Vinnie's advice. He slowly turned his head and slid it back. His head popped free! Bolt fell back, relieved. Suddenly, he noticed one of those small pink packing peanuts still stuck to his fur. He tried to shake it off. "What are these things?" he asked, remembering his ride in the cardboard box. "They've weakened me—"

Vinnie cut Bolt off by telling him they were harmless. But Bolt only became more suspicious.

"This has the green-eyed man written all over it! Have you seen the man with the green eye?" Bolt asked.

Vinnie stared back at Bolt, then nodded at his pigeon buddies. "You know, I gotta say something, if I could say something here," he finally said to Bolt. "You look familiar."

Vinnie turned to Joey. "Hey, look at this guy's mug!"

"Yeah, yeah," Joey said, shaking his head. "You know, I could have sworn I seen this guy before."

Behind them a bus zoomed by with a giant ad for the *Bolt* TV series on the side. The pigeons didn't notice it. They were too focused on the dog in front of them.

"Yeah," Bobby, the third pigeon, agreed. "Hey, you ever hang out on Fourteenth Street with a stray named Kelvin?"

"Yeah," Joey said, "Kelvin the labradoodle!"

"What?" Bolt said, annoyed, knowing they were wasting precious time. "No! Listen! The man with the green eye! Tell me what you know, birds!"

Vinnie kept looking at Bolt's face. "You gotta give me something here," he said, "because this is ridonculous!"

"Absolutely ridonculous," Bobby agreed.

"*Capisce ridonculous?*" Vinnie asked Bolt. "You know what that means?"

"You pigeons are useless!" Bolt turned to go. "I need someone on the inside. Someone close to the green-eyed man. A cat!" Bolt finally said, thinking all cats must know the evil Dr. Calico.

Vinnie's beady eyes lit up. "Whoa, a cat?"

"Yeah, a cat," Bolt snapped, "and when I find him, whoaooo-ooo-ooo!" He punched his paw at the air. "When I find him, I'm gonna make that cat wish he was never born."

Vinnie turned to his buddies and gave them a wicked smile. They smiled back. They knew just the cat they wanted Bolt to meet.

Across town, a scrawny alley cat named Mittens was lying on a crate as a procession of pigeons walked up to her, giving her meager offerings of food. Mittens had a rough life. The black cat lived alone on the streets of New York. That meant food was not plentiful. She had to beg, scrounge around in trash cans, and look for scraps. The food Mittens was able to find was always dirty and gross, but Mittens didn't care—just so long as she got some food somewhere. She always seemed to be hungry.

The pigeons had become her best deal yet. She realized that because they were birds and she was a cat, they were terrified of her—well, not so much her as her claws. Birds lived in fear of a cat's claws. So she threatened them into giving her food. The deal was that the pigeons gave Mittens half of their food, and in return, she offered them protection. One pigeon named Saul gave her the small end of a hot dog.

"Okay, Saul. Nice work," Mittens said. "Let's find some mustard next time, okay, babe?"

Ted was next in line. "Is that an everything bagel, Ted? Good for you."

Mittens was pleased with her dealings thus far today. The pigeons were delivering a decent sampling of food in return for protection.

Then Louie arrived with . . . a tiny crumb.

Mittens fumed. "Louie? What is this?"

Shivering with fear, the pigeon replied, "It was a slow week. That's half of what I got."

The silence between the two was interrupted by a low grumble coming from Mittens's stomach. All the pigeons knew the growl and what it meant. It meant that Mittens was hungry. Really hungry.

"You hear this, Louie?" Mittens asked. "I'm starving here. And when the ol' stomach starts talkin', it ain't talkin' to me. It's talkin' to . . . the *claws*."

"Not the claws!" Louie was terrified.

"I'm holding these bad boys back best I can," Mittens said, referring to her claws. "But the thing is, it's not up to me. I'm playing good cop–bad claws here, Louie. But these things got a mind of their own. And I'm picking up a lot of chatter here."

"I'll do better, Mittens," Louie whimpered.

"I hope so. I really do," Mittens said. "I'm rooting for

you, Louie. So I'll talk to the claws. But in exchange, next week *all* your food comes to me."

"B-b-but," Louie stammered. "That's not the deal. I bring you half; you give me protection. That's the deal."

Mittens glowered. "Yeah, well, the deal just expired. Now get lost!"

As Louie backed down the alley, farther away from Mittens, he gained some courage. "Mark my words, Mittens," he said. "One of these days, someone is gonna stand up to you."

"Yeah, I'm really scared," Mittens replied sarcastically. And then, suddenly, Bolt appeared out of the blue and slammed into Mittens.

"You should be!" he shouted.

Bolt shook Mittens, trying to get information from her. "Where is she?" he demanded.

"Ah, okay! Ah, who?" a surprised Mittens replied, wondering what this crazy dog wanted from her.

Bolt shook her harder. "You know why I'm here," he said, convinced that the cat was connected to Dr. Calico—and therefore knew Penny's whereabouts. "Where is she?"

"Okay, okay," Mittens howled. "Look, buddy, I—I don't know what you're getting at, but . . ."

Mittens suddenly heard laughter coming from the rooftop. It was the pigeons from the other side of town.

"C'mon, Mittens," Vinnie called down. "Just tell the guy where she is. Tell the dog and make him happy."

"Yeah, yeah, Mittens," Bobby laughed. "Tell him!"

Mittens was desperate. "Joey, Vinnie, Bobby. My boys. Would you tell the crazy canine that he's got the wrong cat?"

The three pigeons exchanged a look and shouted to Bolt, "You got her, pal!"

"That's her!" Bobby added.

Mittens didn't know what to say. Bolt stared into her eyes. "Looks like we're going to do this the hard way."

Bolt carried Mittens by the scruff of her neck to the nearest bridge and dangled her over the edge. Mittens howled at Bolt for all she was worth. "You're crazy, man!"

The pigeons watched from the railing. "Hey, Joey," Vinnie said. "Did we maybe go too far on this?"

"You kidding?" Joey answered. "This is the best day of my life."

Bolt growled. "You work for the men in black who work with the green-eyed man. They've taken Penny. Where is she?"

"I don't know what you're talking about!" Mittens yelled back.

"This is becoming tiresome, cat. In fact, I feel a yawn coming on."

Mittens squirmed frantically, terrified that Bolt

would open his mouth and drop her onto the highway below. "Okay! Okay! I'll talk! I'll talk! I know where Penny is! They have her! Yes! The men in black! And the guy—the guy with blue eyes."

"Blue eyes?" Bolt asked, tightening his grip.

"Um . . . oh!" Mittens said, knowing she needed to get this right. "Green! Yes! Green! The one with green eyes!"

"You just can't stop lying, cat. It's in the genes. It's in your bloodline. It's just gross."

"I know," Mittens said, willing to agree with anything. "It's disgusting. I disgust myself."

She suddenly noticed the tag on Bolt's neck. It had the word HOLLYWOOD on it, along with an address. "But if you put me down," she said, hoping he'd take the bait, "I'll show you where she is!"

"Hmm," Bolt said, carefully weighing his decision.

Moments later, Bolt found himself waiting outside a large trash container behind a restaurant. The restaurant was part of a national chain that made waffles.

"I hope you appreciate the risk I'm taking here," a voice inside the trash bin said. It was Mittens. The end of Bolt's leash was tied tightly around her body. He was taking no chances.

"Every bone in my evil cat body is telling me not to betray the trust of the green-eyed man." She jumped out of the trash, and Bolt watched her spread out a dirty place mat on the pavement. It was a map of the United States with pictures of little waffles showing all the locations of the chain of waffle restaurants.

"Okay," Mittens said. "This is a top-secret map of the entire Earth. Now, here we are," she said, pointing to a waffle symbol in New York, "by the green lady with the big torch. And my boss has Penny locked up. . . ."

She searched the map, looking for the word that matched the address on Bolt's collar. "Ooh! Here!"

Mittens said excitedly, pointing to Hollywood. "By the waffle with the sunglasses! Now all you have to do is get from here to there."

Bolt saw that it didn't seem far from New York to Hollywood on the place mat.

"Well, I told you where to find her, so . . . good times!" Mittens said, grinning and giving Bolt a little salute. She was used to weaseling her way out of difficult situations, but this dog—well, he was downright crazy! "Now, if you'll just untie me, I'll be on my way."

Mittens tugged at the leash. "Wow, that's a good knot. Were you in the navy?" She thought the compliment to the crazy dog might help get her free. A little flattery never hurt, after all.

"Oh, I'll release you, cat. When we find Penny!" Bolt said, pointing to the place mat. Mittens couldn't believe it. She had given this dog all the tools he needed to find this Penny person. This was no longer her problem!

"Excuse me? That wasn't the deal! We had a deal!" she howled.

"Your deal just expired," Bolt replied flatly. There was no way that Bolt was going to give in to an evil minion of Dr. Calico. Mittens was his only hope for finding Penny. She was a cat, and therefore she worked for Calico. She had the means to lead Bolt to Calico's hideout, where he could find and rescue Penny. Until then, the cat would remain his prisoner.

Some of the long-suffering pigeons watched from a clothesline. "The irony," Louie huffed. "She said that to me not ten minutes ago."

With Mittens in tow, Bolt charged down the street. Even though the dog did not have the amazing, scientifically enhanced speed that he thought Penny's father had given him, he was still faster than poor Mittens. The cat clawed and scratched the pavement, desperate to escape, as Bolt ran at top speed.

Meanwhile, a little girl was sitting on a park bench with her mother, who was trying to read a newspaper. The mother was too busy reading to look up.

"Mommy," asked the little girl, "does chocolate cake make you strong?"

"No, honey," the mother answered.

"Is Grandma a robot?" the girl asked.

"No, honey," the mother replied.

"Do doggies walk kitty cats?"

"No, honey," the mother said, still too absorbed in the newspaper to see what her daughter was seeing: Bolt dragging Mittens down the sidewalk on a leash.

Bolt spotted a moving van parked up the street. There was a big picture of sunny California on its side.

Maybe the van was headed toward Penny!

Bolt dragged Mittens to the back of the truck. "Hmm, padlocked," Bolt said. He opened his eyes wide and stared at the lock hard.

"What are you doing?" Mittens asked Bolt, who seemed to be in a trance.

"Stand back!" Bolt said, not turning. "If I stare at the lock really hard, it will burst into flames and melt."

Mittens took a moment to take this in. "Okay," she said finally. "Now I'm concerned on a number of levels."

They both suddenly heard footsteps approaching. Two college students were carrying a sofa to the back of the truck. "Oh, no! Intruders!" Bolt called out. He rushed for cover, dragging Mittens behind him.

"Whoa!" Mittens cried, bouncing on the pavement. "Owf, owf, slow down, you freak! You're scraping the fur off my—" Mittens suddenly sailed into the side of a mailbox with a *whap!*

Bolt slowly dragged an unconscious Mittens under the mailbox while he watched the two students open the back of the truck. "Oh, boy, this thing is heavy," one of the student movers said.

His partner was huffing as well. "Hey, hey, put it down! I forgot the keys. I'll be right back."

The moving guy collapsed on the sofa as his buddy trotted off.

"Whoo!" he said, glad to rest for a moment. Then a penny suddenly rolled to a stop at his feet.

As he leaned down to pick it up, Bolt sneaked under the couch, dragging Mittens behind him.

"Hey! Lucky penny!" the moving guy said, flipping the coin into the air.

His partner snatched it before it landed. "Thanks," he said. "Now move your butt."

"Okay, let's do it." The first guy grunted as he picked up his end of the sofa. Then they loaded it—with Bolt and Mittens hidden underneath—into the truck.

The pigeons watched the moving van zoom out of the city. Vinnie shook his head in frustration. "Ugh, I know that dog, I'm telling you, Joey."

Far off in the sunny land of Hollywood, Penny sat on Bolt's bed and cried.

Her agent burst into the trailer. "I've got great news!" he exclaimed.

"Really?" Penny perked up, thinking the agent might have found Bolt.

"I booked you on a talk show! Lead guest!" her agent said excitedly. Penny's face fell. She had hoped for news about Bolt. She missed him and was worried that he was lost for good.

The agent took one look and changed his tone, trying to sound as if he cared about Bolt: ". . . Which means nothing if Bolt is still missing. It's not even good news. Like, whatever, a talk show."

Penny's mom hugged her. "Aw, it's okay, baby."

"He must be so scared," Penny said.

"Scared? Oh, this is Bolt we're talking about," her mom said, comforting her. "He's not scared of anything!" Penny laughed a little.

Her anxious agent tried a different approach. He was

desperate to get Penny on that talk show! "I bet Bolt would want you to do the show," he said, hoping she would believe him.

It didn't work. Trying to fill the awkward silence, the agent gave Bolt's toy carrot a squeeze.

Penny's mom glared at the agent and then turned to her daughter. "Bolt loves you very much, sweetie," she said to Penny. "And you're here. He couldn't have gone far."

Penny nodded and hugged her mom as the moving van carrying Bolt passed a WELCOME TO OHIO sign thousands of miles away.

Bolt sat in the back of the moving van, on alert, staring at the door. Mittens riffled through boxes, looking for a weapon to use against Bolt. She wanted desperately to escape. Trying to distract Bolt and keep him from seeing what she was doing, Mittens struck up a conversation. She pretended that she believed his crazy story about being some kind of amazing hero with special powers.

"So, uh, if you've got these super powers . . . I guess that makes you, like, a super-dog?" Mittens asked, still trying to distract Bolt.

"That information is classified," Bolt replied.

"Oh, c'mon! Like . . . what's your best power?"

"That information is classified," Bolt repeated sternly as Mittens spotted a boomerang in a box and dropped the wrench she had just picked up.

"Can you fly?"

"Don't be silly. I can't fly."

Mittens was plowing through all the boxes. She pulled out a loofah brush and examined it as she continued to distract Bolt.

"Yeah. Silly me," she said. "So, um, if you can't fly, your coolest power is what, again?"

"That information is classified." Bolt remained firm.

Mittens pulled a bowling trophy out of one of the boxes. Whoa! That was heavy. Then she spotted something perfect—a baseball bat! She crawled up a pile of boxes to get to the bat.

"Okay, fine," she said, trying to keep her voice level. "If you don't have any powers, you don't have any powers." Her mind was on that bat.

Bolt continued to stare at the door, alert as always, for the enemy. But he couldn't hold back when Mittens doubted his special powers. "I have a super bark."

"A super bark. Wow." Mittens struggled to pick up the heavy bat. "So what exactly does one do with a super bark?"

"It's classified. I really can't talk about it, so I suggest you just pipe down and take me to Penny."

"You're awfully attached to this Penny character, huh?" Mittens said as she struggled up the back of the sofa with the bat.

"She's my person," Bolt said.

"She's *a* person," Mittens answered, quietly raising the bat over Bolt's head. "And if you ask me, the only good person is, uh—" The weight of the bat suddenly pulled Mittens backward. A stack of boxes tipped over along with her, sending a shower of pink packing peanuts over Bolt.

The dog cried out in a panic and grabbed the truck's door latch. "Tuck and roll!" he yelled to Mittens as he pulled the door open.

"Tuck and what?" Mittens exclaimed, looking out the door of the fast-moving truck.

In an instant, Bolt fearlessly leaped out the door, yanking Mittens along with him.

Bolt and Mittens hit the ground and tumbled to the side of the road. In a cloud of dust, Bolt finally got to his feet.

"Ow!" Bolt cried, raising a foot. "What is this red liquid leaking from my paw?"

Mittens rubbed her head. "It's called blood, hero."

"Do I need it?" Bolt asked. He had never felt this way before, and he certainly had never seen this red stuff.

"Yes!" Mittens shouted. "So if you want to keep it inside your body where it belongs, you should stop jumping off trucks doing eighty on the interstate!"

"Yeah, normally I'm a tad more indestructible."

He spotted one of the pink packing peanuts on the ground and sprang back, panicking. "That stuff! It—it weakens me."

Mittens finally saw her chance. She dove for the pink peanut and waved it in front of Bolt's nose. "Aha!" she said giddily.

Bolt froze. "What are you doing, evil cat?"

"All right. That's it," Mittens said. "I've had it with you! Untie me, pooch, or I'm gonna seriously wound you." She took a breath and gave it her best bluff.

Bolt was horrified. "Are you mad?"

"Oh, yeah, I'm mad," Mittens said as she and Bolt slowly circled each other.

Bolt cowered. "Agh! Okay, cat! You win. I'll untie you."

Then out of nowhere, Bolt said, "That's a weird place to put a piano."

Mittens turned—there was no piano. His ploy worked! Bolt grabbed the chance.

"Hee-ya!" he yelled, giving her paw a karate chop. Mittens dropped the peanut, and Bolt clutched her scrawny neck in his teeth. "Are we gonna have any more problems, cat?"

"No, no, we're cool! We're cool! I'll take you to Penny!" Mittens said, gasping.

A delicious smell suddenly wafted in their direction. Bolt's stomach roared violently. Completely caught off guard, Bolt started to panic. This was another feeling he had never experienced before: hunger.

Grabbing his stomach, Bolt shouted at Mittens, "What is that?"

"What?" Mittens grumbled.

Bolt's stomach growled again. He was shocked.

"THAT!" he shouted. "There are sounds, horrible sounds, coming from my stomach region." Bolt looked at his belly. "There it is again! Oh, you have two seconds to tell me what you've implanted in me, cat! Uh, poison? A parasite? Uh, poison? Oh, wait. I said that already. I can't even think!"

"I don't believe this." Mittens rolled her eyes. "You're hungry."

"Where's the antidote?" Bolt cried, desperate to know how to undo this strange feeling—this thing— Mittens had put in his belly.

"Okay! Okay!" Mittens walked up over a hill and saw an RV park filled with people cooking. "There's your antidote: food."

Bolt heard the wonderful sound of meat sizzling on the grill. The aroma of steaks and burgers was everywhere!

"Go on!" Mittens told Bolt. "Use the dog face. You know . . . beg?"

"What are you talking about?" asked Bolt.

Mittens couldn't stand it. "Figures. I'm tied to the one dog on Earth who doesn't know how to beg." Taking a deep breath, she began coaching Bolt. "Okay, if you want foo—the 'antidote,' you're going to have to do exactly what I say."

"Pssh! Not likely!" Bolt grasped his stomach. "You're a degenerate creature of darkness. The day I listen to a cat is the day . . ." Bolt toppled over, clutching his belly as it roared again. He had to give in.

"All right!" he agreed.

"Great!" said Mittens. "Now, what I want you to do is . . . hmm, tilt your head a little. More, more," she said, coaching Bolt into looking irresistibly cute.

"This is stupid," Bolt complained.

"No, no, no, no, no. C'mon, work with me on this,"

Mittens pleaded. She was hungry, too. "Please. You're almost there."

"Oh, boy," Bolt said, sighing and tilting his head to the side.

"Now a little smile."

Bolt gave a halfhearted attempt at a smile. "Nah, lose the smile. Drop your left ear." Bolt lowered his right ear. "Your other left," Mittens corrected.

"Okay," she sighed. "The other way was better. Now drop them both." Mittens knew they were close. "Hold it right there. Now, ever so slightly, look up."

Mittens marveled at her own genius. Bolt looked sweetly helpless. He had the perfect dog face.

"Soup is on, baby!" she said triumphantly and led him into the RV park.

An elderly couple was sitting in their RV about to have dinner when they heard a whimpering sound. They opened the door to find Bolt staring up at them. Mittens hid and watched the couple coo over Bolt. Finally, they tossed him a bit of food.

Bolt and Penny play action heroes
on TV—but Bolt thinks
their adventures are real!

Bolt accidentally gets shipped to
New York. He thinks a portable
toilet is where Dr. Calico has
trapped Penny.

Three New York pigeons think Bolt looks familiar. They don't recognize him as a famous TV-show dog.

The pigeons tell Bolt where he can find a cat named Mittens.

Mittens teaches Bolt the "dog face."
She explains that if he looks
cute, people will give him food.

Bolt's "dog face" melts people's hearts. He gets enough food scraps for himself and Mittens.

Rhino the hamster
loves Bolt's TV show. He's
Bolt's biggest fan!

Bolt prepares Rhino for their
mission. He tells the hamster that
the road will be rough.

"Let it begin! Let it begin!"
Rhino is ready for some action.

Bolt realizes that he doesn't have
any amazing powers, but Rhino still
believes that Bolt is a super-dog.

Bolt and Rhino find the animal
shelter where Mittens is trapped.

Bolt and Rhino attempt a
daring rescue to free Mittens.

Mittens pumped her fist in triumph. "Yes!"

She had Bolt hit up every RV in the park. He rolled over. He rubbed his back on the ground. He panted. Each cute expression was better than the last. Every trick got an "Aww!" from the campers and a small scrap of their dinner. All those little scraps were adding up to a full supper!

Inside another RV, the voices from a TV soap opera filled the trailer. "I want to know what happened at Big Bear," an actress said.

"And why does that matter to you?"

"Because I'm involved with James. If you and James were romantic, I want to know about it."

"What? So you can—" The channel changed, and a game-show host yelled, "C'mon down!"

The channel changed again.

In front of the TV, a fat little hamster in a plastic ball rolled on the remote again. "It's six-eleven," a TV anchorman said. "Time for the weather."

The hamster kept rolling on the remote, hoping to find something good to watch. Finally, the hamster squeaked, delighted to have found an action show. He sat back and stuck a wood chip in his mouth.

Outside the trailer, Bolt began to bark and whimper. An elderly woman opened the door and smiled. "Well, would you look at that?" she said. "Hello, puppy. Did you come for some of Grandma's butter-bean dumplings? You wait right there and I'll be back with some, okay?"

The hamster rolled to the window to see what all the commotion was about. In the background, the TV played on. But the hamster wasn't listening. His favorite action hero was right outside his window!

Mittens sat next to Bolt at a picnic table. "Look at you," she said. "You're quite the little actor, huh?" She patted her tummy. "Oh, man, I haven't eaten this well in ages. My stomach's distended! How great is that?"

"Don't get used to it," Bolt said seriously. "We have to keep moving."

"But c'mon! This place is a gold mine!" Mittens said. "Every week, new RVs bring us new suckers who bring us new food. Look around! It's perfect!"

The sound of a plastic ball bouncing onto the picnic table suddenly caught their attention. Inside the clear ball, a fat little hamster was exclaiming, "Do my eyes deceive me? Is this some apparition I see before me? Or could it be . . . my hero?"

The hamster rolled down onto the bench attached to the picnic table as Bolt and Mittens stared.

"Oh, my gosh! Oh, my gosh! Oh, my gosh! You're Bolt the super-dog! You're fully awesome!" The wide-eyed hamster squealed in utter glee. "Oh, hohoho!"

"Wait a minute," Mittens said. She could not believe

that the hamster recognized Bolt. "You know this dog?"

"Oh, I do, I do. He's awesome! I mean, he's fully awesome!"

"Uh, yeah," Mittens said. "We've established that. Who are you?"

"I'm Rhino," the hamster answered proudly.

Mittens raised an eyebrow. "Rhino . . . the hamster?"

"Well, you know, my ancestry isn't all hamster. I'm one-sixteenth wolf, with a little wolverine in there somewhere. But that's beside the point. What we have before us is a legend—BOLT!"

Rhino raced back and forth in his ball. "He can outrun speeding missiles! And burn through solid metal with his heat vision! Ooh, oh! And best of all," he said excitedly, "he can obliterate large structures with his bark!"

"Wait a minute," Mittens said, not believing a word. "You've seen his super bark?"

But before Rhino could respond, Bolt interrupted. This sounded suspicious! "Have you been observing me?" he accused Rhino.

"Oh, yeah!" Rhino answered enthusiastically. "I watch you all the time!"

"That's incredible." Bolt was shocked. How could Rhino know about all his secret missions?

"Oh, it's nothing, really." Rhino shrugged.

Bolt turned to Mittens. "But I'm so vigilant. No one can evade my detection!" Bolt looked at the hamster. "You're a phantom!" he exclaimed.

Mittens rolled her eyes.

"Uh, if you say so," Rhino replied. Then he spun around and showed them the big blotch of a birthmark on his side. "Check it out!" he said, pointing to the dark blob. "Take a gander at this Bolt action!" The blotch looked nothing like the lightning bolt on Bolt's side. "Scary, huh? It's like we're twins!" Rhino said proudly.

Mittens looked at the hamster as if he were completely insane. "Yeah," she said, "scary."

The little rodent turned toward Bolt. "So where's Penny?" he asked.

"She was kidnapped by the green-eyed man," Bolt replied grimly.

"Kidnapped?" Rhino said in alarm, rolling in circles on the picnic bench. "The green-eyed man? This is terrible! She could be in grave—"

Bolt stopped Rhino's ball. "Grave danger, I know. But I've captured this cat."

Rhino glared at poor Mittens. "An agent of the green-eyed man, I presume?"

"Oh, you presume correctly," Bolt replied. "She's taking me to Penny."

Rhino turned his tiny eyes toward Mittens. "You . . .

69

you are vile vermin! How do you sleep at night?" he asked with disdain.

"Penny is the most wonderful person in the world!" Rhino went on, waving his tiny arms. "And she loves Bolt. And he's awesome. And you're a monster! How dare you disrupt their relationship with your evil? Die! Die!" Rhino screamed as he launched himself off the picnic bench and straight toward Mittens.

Bolt grabbed the ball, stopping Rhino.

Rhino scrambled against the plastic ball's sides. "I can take her, Bolty!" he said, his feet scurrying in a blur. "Lemme at her! Die! Die!"

"Whoa, whoa, easy. Easy, Rhino," Bolt said.

"You're right," the hamster said, panting. "We need her alive."

"Ah . . . 'We'?" Mittens asked.

"Yes," Rhino said with fierce determination. "Bolt, I could be a valuable addition to your team."

"I'm listening," Bolt said, leaning forward.

"I'm lightning-quick, and I have razor-sharp reflexes." The little hamster demonstrated a few jujitsu moves inside his ball. "And I'm a master of stealth," he added. "Plus I'll keep the cat in check." Rhino shot Mittens a nasty look.

Bolt looked closely at Rhino's ball.

"The road will be rough," Bolt said, warning him.

"I have a ball," Rhino replied.

"There's no turning back," Bolt said, inching closer to Rhino.

"Guess I'll have to roll with the punches," Rhino said smoothly. The hamster was ready.

"Easy won't be part of the equation," Bolt said, still trying to challenge him.

"Promise?" Rhino stared Bolt right in the eye.

"Gotta warn you, we're going into the belly of the beast. Danger at every turn," Bolt said gravely.

Rhino scoffed. "I eat danger for breakfast."

"You hungry?" Bolt asked, making sure the hamster could take it.

Rhino puffed out his chest and cracked his neck dramatically. "Starving!"

"Welcome aboard!" Bolt told the ecstatic hamster.

Mittens tapped Bolt on the shoulder.

"Um, hey, can we talk for a second?" Mittens whispered to Bolt. "I don't know what's going on here, but I'm just a little concerned about the number of lunatics on this trip. My limit is one."

"He's coming with us," Bolt replied.

Mittens was about to argue when Rhino rolled up, hitting his ball against her leg. "Move it, prisoner. We're losing daylight!"

Bolt nodded to his new sidekick and looked out

across the countryside. "I agree. We need to find a fast set of wheels."

"I've got a better idea," Rhino said. "Follow me."

The hamster began to roll off in his ball.

Bolt followed Rhino, dragging a reluctant Mittens behind him.

Moments later, the trio was on an overpass, looking down at a train speeding out of a dark tunnel.

"All right. Give the target a quick flyover, adjust trajectory, and land dead center," Bolt said. "Am I missing anything, Rhino?"

"Just the knowledge that every minute spent in your company becomes the new greatest minute of my life!"

Mittens knew what they were planning. "No, uh-uh! Forget it!" she yelled, clawing at the ground and tugging at the leash that connected her to Bolt. "How do you say 'No way I'm doing this' in crazy?"

"Calm down, cat, you're with me," Bolt said.

"That's the problem!" she yelled as she watched Bolt tug on a local high school's homecoming banner draped over the bridge.

Mittens was filled with terror. "Oh, would you relax?" Rhino said. "Every time he did this on the magic box, it was awesome."

Mittens stopped pulling at the leash. Rhino had

gotten her attention. "Magic *what*?" she snapped.

"You know, the magic box people stare at?"

Mittens couldn't believe what she was hearing. She closed her eyes. "Does this 'magic box' have moving pictures on it?"

"Yeah!" Rhino answered eagerly. "And Bolt's pictures are the best!"

"Bolt's pictures . . . of course!" she yelled, certain now that the idiot hamster was talking about a TV set. "They're not real! He's from—" But before she could say the word *television*, Bolt started to make his move.

"Oh, no! No! Wait! Bolt! Dog! Hear me out!" Mittens pleaded.

Bolt moved into position as the next speeding train zoomed underneath them.

"Let it begin! Let it begin!" Rhino chanted, ready for the first big adventure of his life.

Bolt grabbed hold of the flimsy banner with his teeth. "Wait!" Mittens screamed as Bolt leaped off the overpass. "You are not a super—" But her words were lost in the air that rushed past them as they swung toward the moving train.

For a second, it looked like a special-effects stunt worthy of Bolt the TV hero. But the banner's rope suddenly pulled loose. Instead of landing gracefully on top of the train, they were heading right for the side of it! Bolt, Mittens, and Rhino braced themselves.

Luckily, the tall freight cars were followed by empty flatbed cars, so the three animals avoided a full-on crash as they swung across the train. Bolt was shocked—they were *supposed* to land on top of the train. He was even more surprised when they began to swing backward toward the train's side again.

He let go of the banner, and the three of them went flying through the air. They landed on top of the fast-moving train.

Bolt could see Rhino's ball bouncing along the train's metal roof as he tumbled and struggled to his feet. Rhino was running with all his might to avoid falling off the train's roof.

Mittens was thrown to the back end of the train. She was hanging from the train's ladder, holding on with everything she had.

Bolt made his way toward her, yelling, "Mittens! Mittens, take my paw! I need you alive!"

"You're crazy!" Mittens screamed back. "Stay away from me!"

"Take my paw!" Bolt shouted, climbing onto the ladder to reach her. "I'll save you!"

"No, you won't! You're not really a super—"

Bolt's weight suddenly caused the ladder to tumble over. Mittens screamed as she and Bolt fell toward the train tracks. They were now only inches above the ground, clinging to the ladder, which had extended beyond the end of the train.

Mittens quickly scurried across the ladder to try to grab hold of the back of the train. But Bolt simply couldn't move. His collar was caught on the ladder!

Mittens could see that the ladder was hanging from the train by only two screws, and one of them was popping loose. If the ladder broke, she would fall, too. She was still leashed to Bolt. Mittens simply had no choice. She had to help Bolt.

From his plastic ball atop the train car, Rhino watched the evil cat. Certain that she was tampering with the ladder, he snarled, "Saboteur!" Then he bravely jumped down onto the train's platform and tried to knock Mittens away.

"Ouch! You moron! Stop it! I'm trying to help him!" Mittens shouted, straining to hold a screw in place. The screw was barely keeping the ladder attached to the speeding train.

"Help him?" Rhino yelled, rolling into her again. "Help him? Yeah, right!"

Mittens noticed the other screw coming loose. The ladder was going to fall in no time. She leaped onto the other screw, nearly knocking Rhino off the train.

"Don't worry, Bolt!" Rhino shouted with gusto,

rolling toward Mittens again. "I'll stop her!"

As Mittens struggled, the first screw popped out. Now the ladder was hanging on by only one wobbly screw, and Bolt still couldn't get his collar free!

The train rolled around a bend and the ladder swung out. A post next to the tracks was coming up fast. Bolt was about to smash into it. He struggled with his collar as Mittens put all her weight into holding the last screw in place.

"I can't hold it. BOLT!" Mittens screamed.

"Let go, you monster!" Rhino attacked Mittens.

Bolt's collar suddenly broke free. The momentum sent him flying toward Mittens and Rhino. All three hurtled off the train, just before the ladder smashed into the railroad crossing pole.

Mittens found herself tumbling down a hillside in the middle of nowhere. Bolt smashed through some trash cans and landed with his back against a tree. "Oh, ow, ow!" he cried as he painfully got to his feet.

Mittens took this opportunity to climb a tree. Bolt would have a much harder time dragging her around with the leash that still kept them tied to each other.

"The real world hurts, doesn't it?" Mittens asked from the tree. "But you wouldn't know about that, would ya?"

Bolt looked up. "Get down here, cat! We don't have time for this."

"I'll get a ladder," Rhino said, and rolled away, enthusiastic as ever after the thrill ride he had just taken with his hero.

"Look, genius," Mittens said, safe from Bolt's reach. "You are part of a TV show. You know what that is? Television? It's entertainment for people. It's fake! Nothing you think is real, is real!"

"That's preposterous!" Bolt answered.

"Think about it, Bolt," Mittens said. "Since you got lost, none of your powers have been working, have they? **For the** first time, you're hungry. You're bleeding. I mean, do you really think you were born with a birthmark in the exact shape of a lightning bolt?"

"It's my mark of power, cat," Bolt replied.

"It's the mark of a makeup artist, dog!"

"You're ridiculous!" Bolt was getting frustrated. "Now, get down here!"

"No." Mittens sat firmly on her tree limb, wrapping the leash tightly around a branch.

"Mittens . . ." Bolt tried to control his temper, but he couldn't help himself. He threatened to use his super bark to get her out of the tree.

"Go nuts," Mittens challenged the dog.

Bolt took the stance for a super bark. "You leave me no choice." Then he let loose a loud bark.

Nothing happened. Bolt was stunned. Mittens was not. She knew Bolt had no amazing bark.

"Oh, the super bark," she said sarcastically as she lay back on the branch, completely relaxed and unworried.

Bolt barked again.

"Okay, you can stop now," Mittens shouted above Bolt's barking. "That's enough!"

Bolt's bark didn't blow Mittens out of the tree, but it did attract attention. An animal-control truck pulled up.

"Be quiet!" Mittens yelled at Bolt. Then, in a lower voice, she added, "Bolt, we gotta run!"

Bolt kept barking at the tree until the animal-control officer grabbed him by the collar and tossed him into the back of the truck.

The man reached up to the tree branch, grabbed Mittens, and locked her in a separate enclosure in the truck. The metal doors slammed shut, leaving Bolt and Mittens in darkness.

Just then, Rhino rolled up with the ladder he had promised to get. He watched as the truck faded off into the distance.

On a studio lot in California, Penny and her mom were busy copying LOST DOG flyers inside one of the soundstages. Penny looked up when she heard her agent call.

"Look who we found, young lady!" The agent was carrying Bolt's crate. "It's Bolt! They found him! Just like I promised."

Penny was overwhelmed with joy—until the dog exited the carrier.

"It's not him," she said, staring at the Bolt look-alike headed toward her.

Before the new Bolt got to Penny, there was a clicking sound. An animal trainer appeared. The new Bolt stopped immediately when he heard the sound of the trainer's clicker.

"Well, that depends on how you look at it." Penny's agent tried to turn the awkward situation around. "You know, when I was little, I wanted a bicycle for my birthday. But my parents got me a baseball glove. So you know what I did? I pretended that the baseball glove was a bicycle, and I rode it to school."

Penny stared blankly at the agent in disbelief.

Mindy-from-the-network entered the room. Penny looked into her eyes. "Look, kid, it's time we were honest with you," Mindy said, getting straight to the point. "If we don't get back into production, people are going to lose their jobs. Good people. With families."

Penny listened carefully. She didn't want people with families to lose their jobs. "But Bolt—" she tried to say.

Mindy quickly put her arm around Penny. "We feel for you," she said, trying to make the girl understand. "We loved that dog, too. And the last thing we wanna do is ask a little girl to make a grown-up decision. But it's come to that. We need you to move on. We need you to let Bolt go."

Penny looked at the new Bolt. He was cute, and he wagged his tail. She had no choice.

Slowly, Penny reached over and pressed the Stop button on the copy machine. No more LOST DOG flyers would be made today.

Far away, inside an animal-control truck, the dogcatcher sipped his coffee and headed for the pound. In the back of the truck, Bolt shook his cage. "Arrgh!" he shouted, exhausting himself. He thought the door must be made of the same stuff as those packing peanuts that had weakened him.

Mittens could hear him from inside her cage. "No! No, please! I can't end like this!" She clawed helplessly at her own door, trying desperately to get out.

"Stop worrying, cat. I'll get us out of here!"

Mittens looked up. "You can't, Bolt! You got nothing!" Bolt had to learn that he did not have amazing powers that could save them.

Bolt concentrated on the door. He was convinced that his heat vision would work.

"Listen to me," Mittens pleaded. "We are being taken to a place where humans go animal shopping. Now, they pick the cute ones—the ones that look like you. But the rest never come back out."

"I said I'd get us out of here, all right?" Bolt said, deciding to try his best burst-through-the-door move. He backed up, lunged forward, and rammed his head into the metal door. *Ouch!* He fell back, the door still firmly in place.

"Ugh! My hero!" Mittens said sarcastically as the truck bumped down the road and pulled into a gas station. As the truck idled at the pump, a plastic ball rolled in behind it.

Rhino was in high spirits. "Ring, ring, who is it?"

Rhino said to himself. "Destiny?" He laughed. "I've been waiting for your call!"

He twisted the escape hatch of his ball and slowly emerged, laughing maniacally, preparing for battle. Quickly, the little warrior lowered one foot to the ground, then the other. He was off to save his hero—Bolt!

As Rhino neared the truck, he saw the driver filling the tank with fuel. Rhino laughed maniacally again—in his excited mind, he could do no wrong.

Rhino clambered onto the truck's roof before it pulled out of the gas station. He believed with all his heart that he was on a mission—a very serious mission. He would save Bolt, help Bolt defeat Dr. Calico, and then . . . save the world!

Right now, though, he was in the awkward position of trying to climb down from the truck's roof to reach the hinge on Bolt's cage. Rhino flipped down the side of the truck, grabbing on wherever he could, until he found what he was looking for. Rhino opened the door lever.

Inside, Bolt staggered to his feet, ready to take another run at the cage door.

"Would you give it up already?" Mittens said, resigned to going to the pokey. "You're liquefying whatever brains you have left!"

Bolt reared back and lowered his head. "I cannot be contained in any container!" he shouted, and charged the door.

Bolt sailed through the unlocked door, sending himself and Rhino tumbling onto the road's shoulder just as the truck rumbled away.

Bolt jumped to his feet. "I did it!" he said, stunned. "I'm back!" Bolt proudly puffed out his chest, thinking his powers had returned.

Suddenly, Rhino popped out of the tall grass, celebrating their great escape: "There's no truck that I know that can keep in Bolt and Rhino!"

"Rhino!" Bolt said. "What are you doing here?"

Rhino gave him a grin. "Oh, nothing. I was just enjoying an evening stroll and thought I'd just . . . POP the hatch on that containment unit!"

"You opened the door?" Bolt felt his heart sink.

Rhino made a little raise-the-roof motion with his paws. "Yes, I did! Be-yoink!" he said proudly.

"Wow, uh . . . ," Bolt stammered, trying to figure out what was going on. "That's great, Rhino."

Rhino turned to leave. "All right, now let's go get the prisoner back."

Bolt didn't move. He looked at the lightning bolt mark on his side. It had started to smudge. Wiping a paw over the mark, he watched the black ink rub off.

"I can't," he said sadly to Rhino, realizing at last that his life as a super-dog had been fake.

The pumped-up hamster was already on his way down the road, but he turned around and ran back to Bolt. He climbed onto a fence post, eye to eye with his hero.

But Bolt couldn't face his little friend. This was it. Bolt had finally realized that he had no amazing strength, no super bark, no heat vision. Maybe Mittens was right. Maybe he was just . . . a regular dog. "I—I can't do it," Bolt said, avoiding Rhino's gaze.

"Who are you?" Rhino demanded.

Bolt looked down. This was the lowest point in his life. He didn't know who he was anymore, but he certainly wasn't a hero to anyone, including Penny. "Rhino, you don't understand—"

"You are Bolt!" the hamster interrupted. "The most awesome hero to ever grace Earth's glorious battlefield!"

Bolt nodded weakly. "But I'm not—"

"Who single-handedly destroyed the green-eyed man's undersea lab?" Rhino demanded.

"Me?" Bolt questioned weakly, then objected: "But none of it was—"

"And who barked his army of dog-seeking hover-bots into oblivion? Who? Who, Bolt? Who?"

"Me! But none of it was—" Bolt raised his head.

"You!" the amped-up little hamster exclaimed. "You did, Bolt!"

Rhino turned Bolt's head toward the night sky's shooting stars. "Because all over this planet, there are animals who feel like they can't. Like a little hamster who once dreamt of the day when he, too, would save a little girl from danger and be told 'You did it. You did it, Rhino. You saved the day again.' They need a hero, Bolt! Someone who, no matter what the odds, will do what's right."

Bolt stood still, struck by Rhino's words.

"They need a hero to tell them that sometimes the impossible can become possible if you're awesome!" Rhino squealed with delight. "I'll go get my ball."

And even though Bolt now knew for sure that he was nothing special, he also knew that it was his duty to do what was right. And that meant he had to go save Mittens!

As Rhino cheerily hummed the *Bolt* TV show theme song, he and Bolt marched down a forested road. Over a hill, they spotted a cement-block structure. It was the pound.

Rhino was so excited, his breath fogged up his ball. "This'll be just like the time you infiltrated Calico's artic hover base!" he whispered loudly to Bolt.

Bolt looked at the animal shelter. "It's not going to be exactly like that, Rhino. We're going to have to do things a little differently." Bolt didn't have the heart to tell Rhino that he really had no amazing powers.

Rhino rubbed two small patches clear on the inside of his foggy ball and nodded eagerly. "Oh, stealth mode," he said, adding a smile under the two circles he had rubbed clear.

Inside the animal shelter, an employee named Lloyd was heading out the door. He waved to the woman at the front desk. "Good night, Ester."

"Night, Lloyd," she answered, not even looking up from her computer.

A moment later, the automatic doors of the shelter opened and closed again. "Lloyd?" Ester said, gazing up. But no one answered.

Ester got up to investigate, muttering, "Lloyd, you jump out and scare me, and I'm gonna pepper-spray ya again." She shook her head as she made her way toward the doors. "I swear, it's like working with toddlers."

Rhino and Bolt sprang out from behind the desk. "Threat nullified," Rhino noted.

Quickly and quietly, Rhino and Bolt made their way through the animal shelter. "I feel alive!" Rhino said a little too loudly as he rolled his ball to a stop around a corner.

"Shhh," Bolt whispered, putting his paw on Rhino's ball as if to cover Rhino's mouth. Bolt crossed the hallway and looked inside the cat room. A man sat near the door, reading a magazine.

"There's a guard," Bolt said to Rhino.

Rhino rolled toward the guard. "I'll snap his neck."

Bolt put a paw on the ball. "We need to get him away from that door." Bolt looked around and saw an area marked DOG KENNEL. He had an idea.

Bolt rolled Rhino's ball into the room. The dogs all cried out excitedly: "Ball! Ball! Ball! Ball!" Every one of them was clamoring to get ahold of that ball.

Martin, the guard from the cat room, heard the dogs

barking and wondered what could possibly be causing all the commotion. He left the cat room to quiet the racket. As he walked into the dog kennel, the dogs continued to bark.

"Ahh! Just pipe down!" Martin yelled.

Bolt took advantage of the diversion Rhino was causing and ducked into the cat room. "Mittens? Mittens?" he called out, looking into the cages.

He spotted her scrawny tail sticking out from the cage at the end of the row. Bolt moved closer and saw Mittens cowering and alone. She was shivering with fear.

"Mittens?" Bolt said gently.

Mittens looked up. "Bolt!" The cat was completely surprised. "What are you doing here?"

"I'm busting you out," he replied.

"You—you came back? For me? But you don't have any special powers."

"I know."

"Wow. Crazy day for you, huh?" Mittens looked fondly at Bolt.

"Yes, it has," Bolt admitted. "Are you ready for this?"

"No."

"Me neither." Bolt opened the latch on her cage, and they ran down the hallway together.

Inside the dog kennel, Rhino still had the dogs in a frenzy as they eagerly tried to chase his ball.

"Hey! Hey! Hey!" Martin shouted, moving in closer to investigate the ruckus.

He spotted a dog chewing on Rhino's ball. "Hey, where'd you get that hamster? Give it!" he said, running into the dog's cage.

Bolt stepped into the kennel and barked loudly to let Rhino know it was time to go.

"Hey! Wait!" Martin shouted, trying to scramble to his feet.

Rhino grinned. "Initiating escape," he said as he ran at full speed and propelled his ball, now covered in slobber, out of the dog's mouth and over Martin's head.

Martin yelled, "What the heck?" as he slipped toward Bolt, Mittens, and Rhino, who were making a dash for the shelter's exit.

Just then, Lloyd returned, and Martin spotted him at the end of the hall. Martin shouted, "Lloyd! Block the door! Block the door!"

Rhino screamed with glee, "Super bark! Super bark!"

But Bolt knew he didn't have a super bark. His whole life had been a fairy tale. He felt as if he had been the victim of one big joke. But the next series of events did cause him to bark, and exciting things did happen. . . .

As the animal trio raced toward the exit, Lloyd began to run toward them, causing Bolt and Mittens to slide to a stop. Martin slipped in a puddle of slobber. His feet flew over his head, kicking Rhino's ball toward the exit. As Martin fell to the floor, he landed on Bolt's tail.

"Yarf!" Bolt let out a loud yelp—not exactly a super bark, but a bark nonetheless.

Rhino's plastic ball arced through the air and slammed smack into Lloyd's head. The ball flew toward some balloons that were ready for Animal Adoption Day at the pound. Rhino's ball hit one of the helium tanks, which fell with a clang, snapping off the tank's release valve. Slowly, the gas hissed out of the valve. Then the valve came completely loose and the tank took off like a missile—*whoosh!* It shot through the exit door and hit the animal-shelter sign, breaking it in two.

Bolt and company watched the sign fall into the back of a pickup truck that was carrying a barbecue grill with a propane tank. The tank exploded!

Ester, who had been looking for Lloyd during all this commotion, couldn't believe her eyes.

"What did you do to my new truck?" she yelled.

Amid the uproar, Bolt, Mittens, and Rhino saw their chance and took off for the open road.

Lloyd ran out the front doors, shouting, "You hold on right there!"

Startled, Ester screamed. She raised her canister of pepper spray and got him right in the eyes.

Lloyd fell to the ground, moaning, "Golly, Ester! Spicy eyes!"

Moving along in the brush by the highway, Mittens exclaimed desperately, "We need a ride!"

And that was when Rhino saw the headlights of a large flatbed truck carrying half of a modular home coming in their direction.

"I've got a big one!" he shouted, replying to Mittens's comment.

As the truck slowly moved its wide load down the road, Bolt grabbed Rhino's ball in his mouth.

They ran alongside the moving house. Mittens jumped first, through the plastic sheeting that covered the open half of the house. Bolt leaped in behind her. Rhino's ball rolled out of Bolt's mouth as Mittens and Bolt leaned against a wall, trying to catch their breath. Inside the half-house, they could make out something that almost seemed like a home—or at least half of one. They could see windows and doors, floors with carpet, and kitchen cabinets. The plastic sheeting was protecting the place where the other half of the house would fit.

"I can't believe it!" Rhino chattered. "My whole life I

wanted to see a real, live super bark! Best. Day. Ever!" he said, rolling off to investigate the house.

Bolt slumped against the wall, tired and still trying to come to terms with the fact that he was just an ordinary dog.

"Mittens," he asked quietly, "if I don't chase bad guys, then what am I? I mean what . . ." Bolt let out an anguished sigh.

"Aw," Mittens said. "Don't worry about it. Being a regular dog is the greatest gig in the world." She leaned over to Bolt and whispered, "Look, I'm gonna let you in on a little-known cat secret. You know why we hate dogs? Because we wanna *be* dogs. We have dog complexes."

"But—but what do dogs do?" Bolt asked, feeling completely lost.

"It's a piece of cake," Mittens said, comforting Bolt. "Slobber, sleep, chase tails, and chew shoes. You don't exactly need a master's degree. You know, most dogs live in a place like this—and, uh, do things like . . ."

She wandered into the bathroom. Bolt followed her as she explained that this was where dogs drank. They both looked into the toilet bowl. "Out of this?" Bolt asked, shocked. Mittens shrugged her shoulders and nodded. Then she led him into the kitchen.

"And this is your dog bowl," Mittens explained.

"What is?" Bolt asked, looking around.

"The entire floor. If it hits the ground, it goes to the hound."

As they walked into the living room, Mittens gestured to the fireplace. "And on cold nights, this is the spot," she told him, indicating that this was a warm and cozy place to curl up.

"You seem to know a lot about these places," Bolt commented, wondering how she had learned so much about these things.

"Yeah, I did my time in one of these places," Mittens said, avoiding eye contact with Bolt. "But I'm more of an alley cat at heart. Sprung out the first chance I got. Never looked back."

Bolt knew that she wasn't telling him the whole story. But before he could say anything, Rhino's shouts echoed through the empty house. He was screaming into an air vent that amplified his voice. "RHINO IS AWESOME! HE'S SO AWESOME! HE'S BEYOND AWESOME! HE'S . . . BE-AWESOME!"

Rhino turned to see Bolt and Mittens staring at him. Their ears were ringing. "Uh, I—I am be-awesome," Rhino said sheepishly.

The air coming through the vent felt good on Bolt's face. He leaned in closer.

"I think it's about time I introduced you to the

regular-dog pièce de résistance," Mittens said, and opened a window. "Stick your head out."

"Why?" Bolt asked.

"Just do it," Mittens replied, and watched as Bolt stuck his head into the breeze.

A look of pleasure spread across his face. "This is awesome!" Bolt said gleefully.

"And stick your tongue out," Mittens told him. Bolt opened his mouth and laughed as the wind rushed by.

"This is totally awesome! Why don't you try it?"

"That's okay," Mittens said with a little smile. "It's, ah, more of a dog thing."

As they traveled across the country, each time the truck stopped, Mittens showed Bolt lots of things dogs liked to do. For Bolt, these became some of the best days he had ever experienced without Penny. Mittens taught him the simple joys of fetching a stick and burying a bone and playing with a sprinkler.

When the house on wheels stopped at one of the waffle restaurants, Rhino got a new paper place mat with the same map Mittens had shown Bolt in New York. They used it to navigate across the country, following the little waffle pictures. They jumped on the backs of apple trucks, semitrucks, and hay trucks. They also stopped to ask some pigeons in the Midwest for directions.

Mittens could see that for the first time in his life, Bolt was enjoying just being a dog. At last he could relax and not worry about Dr. Calico or any other villains, focusing instead on running through real grass, barking in the wind, and getting muddy.

Bolt felt real rain fall on his face for the first time, and he loved it. He enjoyed that rain so much that he didn't even notice that his bolt icon was almost completely washed away.

Bolt didn't even realize or care that he looked messy and dirty by the time they pulled into Las Vegas, the world's capital of discarded food.

Mittens had found a home. She couldn't believe this place, where free food—really good food—lay in piles in trash cans and back alleys. She knew that this was where she and her two friends could stay. She had grown to like Bolt and Rhino. She felt at last that she had a family.

She didn't realize that Bolt was still stuck on finding Penny.

"Psst, Bolt. Bolt," Mittens said. She had been working on a surprise for all of them, but she wanted Bolt to see it first.

"What?" Bolt answered.

"Come on!" Mittens said excitedly. "I got a surprise for ya."

"What is it?" Bolt asked, following her down the alley.

"Just close your eyes!" Leading the way, she took Bolt to the outskirts of town. "Okay, now . . . open!"

Bolt opened his eyes and saw a large old neon hotel sign, tossed aside as trash. It was leaning at just the right angle so that Mittens had been able to place three snug boxes underneath it. These boxes were to be their new home.

"Huh?" Mittens said, nudging Bolt with her scrawny elbow. "Bask in the glow."

Bolt didn't know what to say. "Uh, I . . . ," he began.

"Okay, okay, okay! Just let me give you the grand tour. This one's mine," she said, pointing to the smallest box. She waved her paw at the largest box, which had soft padding at the bottom. "And this one is all yours."

Mittens climbed into the large box and patted the cushion. "I mean, it's not a bed exactly, but it's actually really comfortable!" Mittens looked at Bolt's face. She could tell that he wasn't completely convinced.

"What?" Mittens said, surprised. "I know what you're gonna say: 'Mittens, what if one night I just feel like staying in, curling up with a bone and a book?' Well . . ." Mittens knocked out the pole holding the flap on the box open.

"Ta-dah!" she said, looking at the closed box. "Total privacy. And completely soundproof."

Bolt could tell it wasn't the least bit soundproof, but that wasn't what was bothering him. "Yeah, um . . . ," Bolt began. "Look, I don't think—"

"Okay, I lied," Mittens interrupted. "It's not sound-proof. But we're—"

Bolt stopped her. "Mittens!" he exclaimed, needing her to understand. "I can't stay here!"

"What?" Mittens said, shocked at Bolt's response.

Bolt took a deep breath. "I can't stay here. We're only one waffle away from Penny!"

Mittens couldn't believe it. "You mean you're still going back to her?"

"She's my person," Bolt said simply.

Mittens grabbed Bolt by the ear and yanked him over a small hill that had blocked their view of a huge billboard for the *Bolt* TV show. "Ow! Ow! Ow! Ear! Ear! Ow! Ow!" Bolt yelped.

"Look at me, Bolt. *I'm* real." Mittens pointed at the billboard. "Now, what about this? Huh? Does *this* look real to you?" She pointed at a picture of Dr. Calico, then at a helicopter, then at the laser eyes on the TV Bolt. Finally, she picked a spot on the poster that showed Penny. "How about that, Bolt? She's an actress. She's just pretending. Don't you get it?"

Bolt stared at the picture. "Not Penny." He turned and walked away.

"There is no 'Penny'!" Mittens yelled after him. "She's fake!"

"No! You're wrong!" Bolt shouted back. "She loves me!"

Mittens wouldn't give up. "No, no, Bolt. That's what

they do. They act like they love you. They act like they'll be there forever. And then one day, they'll pack up all of their stuff and move away and take their love with them. And leave their declawed cat behind to fend for herself. They leave her . . . wondering . . . what she did wrong."

Bolt paused and looked back at his angry, hurt friend. He knew that she had finally confessed how she had been abandoned on the streets by her person. "I'm sorry, Mittens. But Penny is different."

Mittens refused to look at Bolt, afraid he might see the tears filling her eyes. "Oh, yeah, sure she is," Mittens said, trying to toughen up. "If you want to go back to her, be my guest. But you're going alone."

Bolt was losing a good friend, and he knew it. But he had to find Penny. She was his person, and he was her pet. "Take care, Mittens," he said sadly as he headed off alone toward Hollywood.

Mittens couldn't tell whether she hated Bolt or whether she had just lost her best friend. Actually, she knew she had just lost her best friend. She also knew that she was furious, because this was the second time she had been deserted.

Mittens was still sad and angry and lonely when Rhino appeared. The hamster was moaning in distress. He had found—and eaten—a bit too much free pizza.

"Hey there, Rhino," Mittens said glumly.

"Morning, cat. Where's Bolt?"

Mittens sighed. "He's gone."

"What?" Rhino gasped. "Without me?"

"Yeah," Mittens said with a shrug. "He wanted me to tell you that he had to face the green-eyed man alone."

Without a word, Rhino spun his ball around.

"Whoa!" Mittens said, watching him roll off. "Where you goin'?"

"To find Bolt," Rhino told her.

"But he doesn't need us anymore!"

Rhino stopped and rolled back toward Mittens. "Trust me. I've seen it a million times before. In the cold, dark night before the battle, when the steely fangs of evil are sharpened and poised to strike, the hero must go and face his greatest challenge . . . alone. But if Bolt has taught me anything, it's that you never abandon a friend in a time of need." Rhino looked determined.

"When your teammate is in trouble, you go," he said, rolling his ball toward the street. "Whether they ask or not, you go. Not knowing if you're coming back dead or alive. You go." He turned right onto the street.

"He went the other way," Mittens said.

Rhino's ball made a quick about-face and headed west. "You go knowing how deep the shrapnel's gonna pierce your hide. But you go."

Sure enough, Mittens watched the little hamster roll away. She turned back to the alley and looked around. For her, it was a paradise, all the food and comfort she could possibly want.

Bolt rode a truck all the way to Los Angeles. He'd had lots of time to think about what Mittens had said. But he knew he was right—Penny's love was real. When he finally arrived in Hollywood, he hopped off the truck. He knew that he was close to finding Penny.

A voice above him said, "No way!"

Bolt looked up to see a pigeon named Blake staring at him. "It *is* you!" Blake exclaimed.

Two other pigeons flew over to join Blake as he began talking rapidly to Bolt. "Bolt! Really big fans of yours, brother. I'm Blake, and this is my writing partner, Tom. Tom, say what's up."

"What's up?" said Tom.

"Oh," Blake continued, gesturing to the third pigeon, "and this is our personal assistant, Billy."

Billy was so starstruck he could hardly speak. "Bolt, I've admired you for so long. I really am your biggest fan, and there's something I've always wanted—"

"Don't talk to him," Blake interrupted. "Go get me some bread crumbs—whole-grain. Go!"

As Billy sadly trudged off, Bolt spoke: "Listen, maybe you guys can help me. I need to find Penny—the girl from my television show. You know where I can find her?"

The pigeons agreed to help Bolt—on one condition: Bolt had to listen to their pitch for an idea for the *Bolt* show.

"It's gonna blow your mind," Tom said.

"Wait for it," Blake added, building the suspense.

"Aliens." Tom seemed quite pleased with himself.

Bolt went along with the idea. So long as the pigeons could take him to Penny, he would listen.

Soon Bolt found himself looking up at the studio gates. He could see the studio's water tower with an image of him and Penny on it. They were hugging. Bolt took a deep breath and walked onto the lot.

At that moment, Mittens and Rhino were just rolling into L.A.

"There it is!" Rhino said, pointing down to the city. "The most terrifying place on Earth."

When he and Mittens finally approached the studio gates, Rhino let out a sinister laugh. "At long last! We've arrived at the belly of the beast—the lair of the green-eyed man!"

Mittens suddenly blocked his ball. "What? What?" Rhino demanded. "What's the problem? I'm pumped!"

"Um, okay, Rhino," she said, knowing that what they were about to see would shatter the little hamster's illusions. "Listen, this may be really hard for you to understand, but, well, you see, sometimes things aren't what they seem . . . exactly."

Just then, a snarling dinosaur statue rolled past them. But Rhino's focus was not on the dinosaur. Rhino saw only one thing—one of Dr. Calico's motorcyclists from Bolt's TV show standing near a catering truck.

Mittens cringed. "And I mean sometimes, things can feel really real when they're not." She looked into Rhino's plastic ball.

"All my training has prepared me for this moment," he said, ignoring everything but the shock trooper. He charged toward his target, yelling, "Die! Die! Die!"

The stuntman who played a shock trooper on the show heard a tiny squeak, looked down, and picked up the plastic ball. "Aw, what a cutie!" he said, staring into the ball.

"I will rip your liver out!" Rhino yelled. But it all

sounded like tiny squeaks to the stuntman.

"Check it out!" the shock trooper said, holding up the plastic ball and peering in at the hamster that was squeaking and wiggling all over the place. "Look at his little whiskers! I had one when I was a kid. I called him Mr. Sparkles!" He looked right at Rhino and said sweetly in baby talk, "You look just like Mr. Sparkles, yes you do!"

Mittens was about to run after Rhino when she saw a flatbed truck go by. It was carrying one of Calico's helicopters. The truck stopped in front of a soundstage with a picture of Bolt on it. Mittens took off after the truck.

Inside the soundstage, Bolt wandered around looking for Penny. Suddenly, he heard her calling, "Bolt! Bolt!"

Bolt raced toward her voice, turned a corner, and entered the set.

Far down a hallway, Penny was crying out, "Bolt? Here, Bolt! Bolt! You're okay!"

Bolt kept running. At last, he was just steps away from Penny, and she did truly love him. She had missed him! He could hear it in her voice!

And then, just as Bolt was about to run out from the shadows and leap into Penny's arms, another dog came dashing across the set. He was white and had a bolt symbol on his side. He jumped right into Penny's arms.

"Oh, Bolt! I thought I lost you!" Penny cried. The real Bolt watched, stunned, as Penny adjusted the new Bolt's collar and kissed the top of his furry head.

"You're my good boy!" she said as she hugged the new dog.

Bolt's heart broke. He had been replaced. And Penny loved the new dog. It really was all fake, just as Mittens had said. He hung his head and left the soundstage. He had nowhere else to go. He had traveled all this way to **find** Penny, only to see that she didn't even care about him.

Behind him, a dog clicker sounded. The new dog on the set ran to his trainer, who rewarded him with a dog biscuit.

"Well, great job, everyone," Mindy-from-the-network said after watching the rehearsal.

"All right," the assistant director announced to the cast and crew. "Let's take a fifteen-minute break and then do it for real."

Penny, tears running down her cheeks, walked over to her mom. "I miss him," she said, sobbing. Penny's mom hugged her. "I know, honey. I do, too."

High above, on a catwalk, Mittens saw the whole thing. She had to find Bolt and tell him she had been wrong. His person really *did* love him!

Bolt walked off the studio lot and into the streets of L.A. He wandered aimlessly past the large posters and billboards advertising his television show.

Bolt just kept walking. He had nowhere to go.

Meanwhile, inside the studio, Penny wiped away her tears as the crew readied her for her next big scene. They fastened her to a harness and a fly cable that would lift her safely into the air. Penny stood on her mark in the middle of Dr. Calico's lair. Fiery torches surrounded the cavernous stone temple to the feline gods.

The scene began with a spotlight on Penny's dad, who was tied to a chair. Elevator doors opened and the evil Dr. Calico stepped out. "Ah, Professor. I'd like to thank you for granting us access to that labyrinthine mind of yours," he said.

Penny's father struggled against the ropes around his wrists. "You've really lost it, Calico. You know I'd never do such a thing."

Dr. Calico slowly petted the cat on his shoulder. "Unless it was the only way to save your little girl's life!" He pointed to a huge fire pit in the center of the temple. Penny was dangling over the flames.

"Penny!"

"Daddy!" Penny cried. Then, looking out through the smoke, she yelled, "Bolt! Here, Bolt!"

"Your dog is nowhere near," Calico said, sneering, when—*SMASH!*—the fake Bolt burst through the doors of the exploding elevator.

"Get that dog!" Calico commanded the shock

troopers guarding his lair. They sprang into action.

They ran toward the new dog with sparks flying from their electrified gloves. It was all too much. The fake Bolt panicked. Terrified, he ran around the set, eventually sliding past one shock trooper and just falling off the platform. The dog knocked a flaming torch to the ground. An entire wall of the set caught fire. The flames started to spread!

Bolt walked down the street, oblivious to the noise and traffic around him. Mittens spotted Bolt and sighed with relief. She had found him.

"Hey!" she cried out, racing to catch up.

"Mittens?" Bolt said, looking up. The last time he'd seen her was in the streets of Las Vegas. "What are you doing here?"

"Long story short: I was tied to a delusional dog and dragged across the country. But that's not important right now. The real question is: What are you doing here? And why aren't you in there?"

"You were right about her, Mittens," Bolt replied, sadly shaking his head. "She—it wasn't real."

"No," Mittens said firmly. She paused as Bolt stared at her, dumbfounded. "No, Bolt, I was wrong. I saw her face. She was devastated. She doesn't want any dog. She loves you." Mittens paused. "She's your person, Bolt. And you are her dog."

"Mittens, be quiet."

"No, no, you need to hear this."

"Seriously," Bolt said as his ears stood up. "Be quiet."

Mittens looked around. "What is it?"

"Penny!" Bolt cried, turning and running back toward the studio.

On the soundstage, flames had spread, and everyone was scrambling to escape the engulfing blaze. Penny dangled helplessly from the cable that held her. "Help!" she screamed as the fire licked her feet. "Please, help!"

Penny looked down through the haze. She saw the air bag beneath her. As sparks fell on her, she quickly brushed them off. She knew she had no choice. She unbuckled her safety harness and fell.

Outside the soundstage, smoke and flames shot into the sky. The shock trooper looked up. In a panic, he dropped Rhino's ball and ran with the rest of the crowd.

Rhino shook his fist at the departing trooper, happy that he had inflicted fear on the pathetic, vile creature— the minion of Dr. Calico.

"Yeah!" the little rodent said to himself, still living the dream. "You better run!" Just then, Bolt and Mittens rushed by. Rhino rolled up to them and exclaimed, "I'm on your six," to let Bolt know his position.

"What do we do?" Mittens asked Bolt frantically.

"Just make sure I get into that building."

The fire-safety official was trying to evacuate the building. "Everyone! Go! Go!"

Bolt courageously ran in the opposite direction, right toward the fire.

Meanwhile, a firefighter pulled Dr. Calico from the building. "Is anyone still in there?" the firefighter asked.

The actor, his face blackened with smoke, coughed. "I don't know!"

A burst of flames suddenly blew everyone back. But a hamster ball moved swiftly through the crowd's feet, following Bolt. No one noticed it in all the commotion. Rhino's ball bounced under some falling debris. A large part of the set fell on the ball, cracking the plastic. "It's a good day to die!" Rhino bellowed fearlessly as the ball continued to crack.

"Not on my watch, rodent!" Mittens said, opening the hatch on Rhino's plastic ball and freeing him just in time.

The entire wall was about to give way. Bolt dashed by them just before the only passage to the soundstage collapsed.

Inside the burning soundstage, Bolt dodged the falling debris. He knew Penny was in there somewhere. He barked and barked, trying to get her attention.

Penny staggered and coughed, but through the roar of the fire, she heard something.

"Help! Please help! Over here!" she shouted.

Bolt appeared on the other side of the soundstage. Bolt and Penny ran toward each other, dodging crumbling, flaming pieces of the set. Nothing could keep them apart now, and nothing did.

Bolt jumped into her arms and Penny hugged him tight. "I knew you'd come back," she said.

A large chunk of the set fell down, starting an avalanche of rubble. In the hazy darkness, the two were separated. Coughing, Penny saw a rope.

She cried out to Bolt in the darkness, "Zoom!"

In an instant the loyal dog was at her side, using the rope to lead her through the fire.

He tried to guide Penny out, but they were trapped. Then Bolt saw an air vent and helped Penny move close to it. He climbed inside, looking for a way out, but realized that Penny was too weak to go any farther. Bolt returned to her and lay down by her side. He refused to leave her.

"Bolt, go!" Penny pleaded. She loved her dog too much. She wanted him to be saved, even if she couldn't be. "I will be all right. Bolt, just go." But Bolt still refused to leave his person—there had to be a way to help her. "You're my good boy," Penny said, nuzzling him. "I love you."

Bolt's ears perked up. He heard sirens through the

vent. He remembered how loud Rhino had sounded when he had yelled into the air vent of the moving house. Bolt put his face close to the vent and barked. The metal vent amplified his bark into one loud boom. He barked again, as loudly as he could. It might not have been a scientifically altered super bark, but it was the best bark Bolt had ever let loose.

Outside, Rhino heard the bark and cheered as a firefighter hacked through the vent.

"I found them!" the firefighter shouted. "They're over here! They're over here!"

Outside the soundstage, an anxious crowd waited. Suddenly, a firefighter burst from the building with Penny slung over his shoulder.

Two paramedics met the firefighter and quickly put Penny on a stretcher. "Coming through! Make a hole!" one of them shouted as they placed an oxygen mask over her face.

Penny struggled to look up. Where was Bolt? Was he okay? Through her blurred vision, she saw another firefighter come out. He was carrying Bolt, who was covered in ash.

"Bolt," Penny said weakly, and his tail began to wag slowly. Penny's voice reassured him that everything was going to be fine now.

Penny laid her head back down. She knew Bolt was okay. She had never forgotten him. He had always been her dog, and she was his person. Now he had rescued her for real—no super powers, no heat vision, no incredible leaps. He had used a simple, normal bark, but he had risked his life to save her. And that normal bark had been far better than any super bark he had done on TV.

Penny's mom pushed through the crowd, desperate to see if her little girl was okay.

"Sweetie!" she said, crying. "You're okay. You're gonna be fine."

The paramedics opened the back of the ambulance and quickly put Penny inside. No one saw that Rhino and Mittens were stowed away beneath her stretcher. They wanted to go with Bolt, and they figured he would be placed inside the ambulance, right next to Penny. They were right!

"I'm so sorry this happened," Penny's mom said to her daughter. A firefighter nestled Bolt beside Penny. Penny's mom let the rescue crew do their job. Then she began to climb into the ambulance to be next to her daughter.

But before Penny's mother could get in, the agent blocked her way and wedged himself inside. It was clear by now that he had no feelings at all for Penny or Bolt. He just cared about making money off them. And this accident was a terrific opportunity for him. A real-life drama like this could provide him with lots of publicity!

"Silver lining!" he said. "She's gonna be fine. This is great PR!"

He flipped his cell phone open and began talking

rapidly, excited by the news. "Felicia! Alert the press! We're on the way to the hospital," he said, hardly even looking at Penny or Bolt.

"Sorry, sir," the firefighter said, interrupting him. "That seat is for relatives only."

"Uh, it's okay. I'm practically family." The agent spoke into the phone again. "Felicia, make sure that they know that—"

"Oh, no you're not! You're fired!" Penny's furious mom interrupted.

"Wait! No, wait!" the agent yelled frantically. "Hey, look! I've got a pin. Let's do this—" But before he could finish his sentence, the ambulance door slammed shut.

Inside the hospital room, a heart monitor beat steadily, flashing a tiny green light on a screen. Penny sat up in bed. Her head was completely covered, wrapped in gauze and bandages.

Slowly, the doctor began the process of peeling them away from her face. "I'm afraid your injuries were more serious than we thought," he said. "We had to completely reconstruct your face."

The doctor removed the last bandage to reveal a very different Penny.

"Take a look," he said, holding up a mirror.

"Well, at least Calico won't be able to recognize me," she said.

In the background, an orderly pushed a food cart into the room. He waited for the doctor to leave, then opened the food warmer. Penny looked up and saw the man holding an ominous green syringe.

"Calico!" she gasped.

He laughed maniacally. But just then, a laser beam

flashed, burning his hand and causing him to drop the needle. Bolt crashed through the window and knocked Dr. Calico to the ground.

"Bolt!" Penny shouted.

With a super bark, Bolt blasted through the hospital walls. But in the next moment, a tractor beam pulled both of them high into the air. Penny screamed as they were drawn skyward into a huge flying saucer.

"Aliens!" Calico shouted.

A TV screen went black. Rhino had rolled over the remote to turn it off.

"This is totally unrealistic," he said, sitting on a sofa in front of the TV.

Bolt leaned in and said, "Absolutely ridonculous."

"You can say that again," Mittens added.

A hand reached out and scratched her neck. "Oh, yeah!" Mittens purred. "Right there! That's the spot!" she said as Penny's mom petted her.

A smiling stuffed carrot suddenly sailed across the room. Bolt's eyes followed it as it bounced onto the couch. He grabbed the carrot, rolled onto his back, and shook the toy from side to side.

Bolt suddenly saw a red-haired girl smiling at him. "Hey, silly dog! Wanna go play outside?" Bolt wagged his tail. "You wanna go outside?" the real-life Penny said, running out of the room. She had quit her TV job, and now she could finally be who she really was: a little girl who loved her dog.

Bolt chased after her as they ran through the yard outside their little farm far, far from Hollywood.

In a tree above them, three pigeons bobbed their heads as they watched Bolt and Penny play. "Does that dog look familiar?" one pigeon asked.

"Nope," the other pigeon answered. "I've never seen him before in my life."

Indeed, Bolt was now a normal dog with a normal life—and it was the best life a dog could have, because he had a person who loved him.